TRAIL
of
MIRACLES

TRAIL
of
MIRACLES

SMADAR HERZFELD

Translated by Aloma Halter

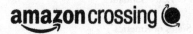

Text copyright © 2014 Smadar Herzfeld
Translation copyright © 2017 Aloma Halter

Previously published as *I, Gittel* by 62 Publishing House in Israel in 2014. Translated from Hebrew by Aloma Halter. First published in English by AmazonCrossing in 2017.

Published by AmazonCrossing, Seattle

www.apub.com

ISBN-13: 9781503943001
ISBN-10: 1503943003

Cover design by Shasti O'Leary Soudant

Printed in the United States of America

TRAIL
of
MIRACLES

My great-grandmother was a tiny, pious woman from a rural village. Behind her house was a chicken coop full of hens and roosters with names like Shaynele, Maydele, and Sheygetz. And the women, it was always women, who slipped into the house or clustered around the chicken coop.

I would look at my great-grandmother, whose name was Gittel, and tell myself that one day I would write a story about her.

Later, she died and later yet, the village in which she had lived also died.

And I forgot.

Years later, in Jerusalem, in the realm of the ultra-Orthodox, I found myself outside a large, ugly building belonging to the Ruzhin Hasidim. And they told me about their sainted Rebbe Yisroel of Ruzhin—how he loved the Holy-One-Blessed-Be-He and how he traveled to Him in a golden chariot, accompanied by servants. And drank his coffee from a cup of the finest porcelain, and walked in shoes stitched from the supplest deerskin. And wore clothes of delicate silk like a sultan. And how, amid all this splendor, he sat and wrote.

~

He loved to tell stories about his grandmother, whom he'd never met. She was called Gittel, and she was the daughter of a renowned Torah scholar, then later, the wife of a famous Hasid.

Her Hasidic husband was called Avraham "the Angel" because he was so ethereal, and there were many stories about him living as if he were not made of flesh and blood, and had no earthly needs. He was the only son of a rabbi and mystic, the great Maggid of Mezeritch. The Maggid himself was known among his disciples as "the talker" in honor of the spirit who talked to him in his mystical revelations.

At twelve years old, Gittel became the daughter-in-law of the Maggid of Mezeritch.

And after just a few years, she was widowed. Though still young, Gittel refused to marry again. She entrusted her two sons to the care of another and set out for Jerusalem, never to return.

All this took place at the close of the eighteenth century.

It was the time of Napoleon, a time of revolutions and conquests, yet in the heart of Europe, there were people who sat on a bench in the shade of trees, pondering the secret life of peas that they grew in their kitchen gardens or dreaming of Jerusalem, the Holy City. At that time, Jerusalem was under Turkish domination.

And it was as remote and forsaken as my great-grandmother herself.

A woman traveling all by herself was rare at that time. Yet tiny Gittel, as stubborn as an ant, made her way all alone toward the east.

Now I sit in Jerusalem, at the very navel of the world, an insignificant novelist of whom only a few have heard.

In my imagination I follow in the footsteps of my great-grand-mother who was also called Gittel and now I'm telling her story.

And Gittel is the grandmother of Rabbi Yisroel, and perhaps my own great-grandmother. And perhaps she's the queen of sorrow and it's simply an old tale.

From my window, I can see a field of peas, and a field of red roses, and the field of time.

Gittel prays and the fish sail on the roof.

And the light is blue.

And the pool is wide and deep.

~

Master of the Universe, help me to be good and wholehearted as I stand before You. Banish the devils from me and drive away my nightmares. I have nothing, nothing apart from the heavy sack of my memories. Like the prophet Jonah, I fled from the land in which I grew up and here I sit at a table, here in the Holy City of Jerusalem, and I write of the things that took place in my life.

Everything that I do now is undertaken in the spirit of prayer. Even scrubbing the laundry and beating it on the washboard is a way of speaking to You. I lower my head before You as I rub the soap up and down. Foam covers my hands, and a slight soughing sound bursts from my throat to the rhythm of my movements. From the day that my husband Avraham the Angel died, I have craved only one thing: to see You, O God.

Although I share not a single trait with the great righteous men, this passionate longing has entered me. Like a grain borne on the wings of the wind, it got into my mouth and spoke from my throat: Give me just one spark of the burning bush, a single moment that will illuminate Your face for me, but may it be for me alone.

I, Gittel, the daughter of the rabbinical genius Meshulum Feivish Horowitz, the daughter-in-law of the great Maggid of Mezeritch, the wife of Avraham the Angel, I remove my outer trappings and stand naked before You.

Gittel, just plain Gittel, is she worthy of seeing Your face?

No one knows me in this place. I have a small room here and a large sink in the yard, where I wash the clothes. I am only a woman, a widow of no standing. Yet, in the darkness of night, Your hand strokes my head and banishes the malevolent spirits that gnaw at my soul.

Since I left my home, my life lurches between noise and silence. Back and forth I move between a large echoing hall to a complete silence that descends inside as into a pool.

Blessed are You, O God, Who enabled me to descend into the pool of the soul and fish inside it for marvels.

Every day in the morning, after I have laid out the wet clothes on the roof, I sit down and enjoy the blue sky. Sometimes the sparrows or seagulls join me, hopping about me, cheeping and pecking at my dress. And I speak to them and laugh with them as if they were my friends.

The air in Jerusalem makes you wise. For days on end I sit doing nothing but inhaling the pure air. This ethereal food makes me feel satiated with sweetness, till I forget to eat real food. From the day I arrived here my body has weakened and fallen prey to disease.

Plagues and diseases are our daily fare in the Land of Israel. Everyone around me is sick, many suffer to the point of death, and entire families are buried in the ground. Sometimes, when I go out, a terrible stench enters my nostrils. Then my stomach turns, my face swells up, and I flee and close myself in my room. When I'm alone, tears burst from my eyes and I cry for hours.

I never cried this way before, with this kind of passion, not even on the day I heard of the death of my son.

Look upon us, O God, cast Your eyes upon the world outspread beneath Your feet and illuminate our path. Love us and redeem our flesh, which decays with hunger and suffering. It is I, Gittel, asking for compassion for Your people, the Children of Israel. May it be Your will to open the Gates of Mercy to us and to give us life in this country. Amen.

The thought of a great Hour of Mercy causes my entire body to shudder. All my life now is longing; my soul burns with a fire that cannot be extinguished and its tongues leap up, licking skyward. The abundance of visions, voices, and dreams overwhelms me and surrounds me with unseen walls. I feel good in the tower in which my soul dwells. The world is reflected to me from the windows, sharp and clear, and I feel compassion for everything: people, animals, plants, and even the stones. All of them so love to live and all of them suffer and die, each in their own way. Why can't it be that all of us live easily and lightly, not suffering, and not dying?

Why can't we live forever?

I read these questions, which have no answers, in the faces of human beings, in the movements of animals, in the beauty of the flowers, and in the endless silence typical of stones. And beyond outward appearances, beautiful or ugly, I see the inner faces and they are filled with pain.

Like a body wrapped in a sheer robe, so is sorrow within happiness, love within hatred, hunger within satiety. And nothing seems simple to me any longer, but one layer over another, a face inside a face.

〜

Once I saw the smile of paradise on the face of a dead butcher. He had always been silent as he cut the meat, and his wife told me that he often heard the voices of cows and hens in his sleep. "Not every person can sleep with blood on his hands," he once explained to his wife. "But with me, the meat comes to me in my dreams and asks me to send it up to heaven."

"He did not know how to say no," his wife lamented. "So when the voices told him that his own hour had come, he lay down in his bed and died quietly."

My heart was suffocating from such intense love, and a great desire stirred within me to peel away the layers, to remove one face after another until I saw the last face. Would it be the smile of paradise or the grimace of hell?

The final moment is the moment of truth, and for anyone who has neither of these expressions on their face, then their life is gone and nothing remains of it. As for them, the faceless dead, I lament them most of all. I see many who are still alive, and they already have, beneath all their faces, a gaping nothingness.

Places too have all kinds of faces. But my life was always a journey to one distant place, enveloped in the glory of legends. Jerusalem. It was the city to which I said my prayers, a king's daughter turned hand-maiden, the City of David that became the City of the Sultan, the secret navel of the world and the place where the gates to paradise are to be found. And when I reached it after much suffering, my heart broke within me and I fell prey to the diseases of humanity. Disappointment seeped into my soul. Why did I insist on coming here? What was I going to do here, in this Vale of Tears, amid scrawny and decaying people, bent and lamenting? I had created a Jerusalem in my mind, but what surrounded me was something else entirely. I could not move and I did not want to move, for there was nowhere for me to go. My body burned with fever and my teeth chattered. My imagination tricked me into thinking I was traveling in a chariot. Sometimes it seemed to me that I was being pursued, and I screamed at the top of my lungs until my voice became hoarse.

Chaya-Rivke, whose husband had died in an epidemic, sat with me in a cold, dark room resembling a cave and instructed her younger children to bring me some water to drink and to recite psalms. From time to time I saw their shadows leaning over me and I heard the faint sound of humming, like angels. Tears fell from my eyes and a feeling of happiness and repose enveloped my limbs. I was sure I was dead and was in paradise.

According to the widow, they truly thought that my soul would soon depart, but suddenly, I grew calmer, and sank into a quiet, deep sleep. I slept for two days deep and strong, and when my senses returned, I did not know where I was and went on lying there with closed eyes. And behind my closed eyelids I saw an angel standing before me, as someone might see at dawn. Slowly, the vision faded, as if the strong sunlight had engulfed it, and only a trace of his presence remained. I breathed in the light-filled air and felt great joy.

A fish cast into the water, a bird released from a cage into the depths of the sky—they know the elation that took me by storm, jolting my each and every limb.

The following morning I got out of bed, reciting the blessing as I washed my hands, and then the Eighteen Benedictions of the Morning Prayer. I was very weak, and when I came to the words *Heal us, O God, and we will be healed,* my legs could hold me no longer and I sank to my knees.

When I reached *He who makes peace upon high,* I shuffled backward on my knees and bowed to the left, then to the right, to the center, and, with a huge effort—as if dragging boulders—I continued a few more moments before collapsing on the floor. Chaya-Rivke's daughter heard the slight noise from my room and hurried in. She kneeled beside me, and I mumbled as loud as I could: *May it be Thy will, O God and God of our fathers, that the Temple be rebuilt speedily and in our time . . .* She waited for me to finish, her dark eyes looking at me with surprise.

"Ah, you've woken up?" She caught me by her cold hands and helped me back to bed. Then she added in a low voice, "So, you're praying? A woman praying . . ." Astonished, she shook her head from side to side.

She was a strange and scrawny creature, pale, and her nose was shiny with oil and red blemishes covered her cheeks. "Don't you have children?" she asked me. Her voice was childlike, but she smelled like an adolescent girl who did not often wash. Apart from this smell, a mustiness hung in the air, and the heavy aroma of spices wafted from the kitchen.

Where I had come from, it was considered unusual for a woman to pray. But here, in Jerusalem? Here women should be throwing open their doors, letting the fresh air inside and praying all day. If that was not so, then why had they come?

The young girl left the room and returned carrying a steaming bowl of buckwheat porridge and sat down to feed me. Her slender fingers held the tin spoon and waited for me to open my mouth, but the effort of praying had affected my mind and I felt that a spider was inching along the spoon and would crawl into my mouth. I clamped my lips shut and moaned like an animal.

"It's only buckwheat," I heard her plead. "We are poor folk and that's all we have to offer. My mother cooked it especially for you . . ."

Her voice pierced my heart and I was overcome with shame. Even if there were a spider, I should not put poor folks to shame. So I closed my eyes and opened my mouth wide. It was warm and soft and as sweet as if it had been cooked in celestial ovens. Over and over again, she brought the spoon to my mouth, and to make it even more pleasurable, she started to sing in a low, hesitant voice that grew more and more confident as she went along.

> *By the roadside there is growing*
> *A rose with azure eyes.*
> *And she pleads with each traveler*
> *Please grant me grace*
> *And raise me from the dust . . .*

And I hummed along with her as I ate. Longing engulfed my soul and I gulped down the food. After the bowl had been emptied, I sank into a slumber. I stroked my sated body and felt it extending, becoming as light as a cloud. I heard the young girl tiptoeing away, and without opening my eyes, I asked her name.

"Sheindel," she whispered.

During my life I have met scores of Sheindels, and yet her name moved me because she was very beautiful in my eyes, just as the name implies. Like this city, she was lowly and wretched, and yet in her heart nestled a fledgling enveloped in the halo of dawn. As if in prayer, I mumbled the names, "Sheindel Jerusalem, Sheindel Jerusalem," and I knew that I had reached the place I had been traveling to all my life.

Those were the days of *selichot*, the prayers that precede the Days of Awe. Every morning before dawn, a fist would knock loudly on Chaya-Rivke's windowpane and her three oldest sons would disappear into the darkness outside. Apart from the banging fist that called people to the synagogue, the reverberating voices of the muezzins echoed from the highest points of the mosques, and on Sundays, the church bells chimed.

Very few Jews lived in the city, and they were hidden like lichen between the ancient stone walls. Most were Sephardim, and the few Ashkenazi Jews who had remained in Jerusalem over the centuries were subject to a double exile, both oppressed by the Ottoman rule and loathed by their proud, superior Sephardic brethren.

O Master of the Universe, how did this land fall so low and become such a place of exile?

On all those days of penitentiary prayers I prostrated myself before God, weeping, and in my heart I cried out, *Whence is the dove that nestled in the Holy City, to where has it vanished? Where is there holiness, O Master—in the Torah ark of the synagogue, in the wind, in good deeds?*

These were my early days in this country. I was still so weak from my sickness, and yet I felt an immense restlessness every day at twilight. I went forth into the alleyways and roamed about. I waited for the grace of a breeze, for a good, cooling wind to caress my lips and disperse my longings. But the air in Jerusalem seemed not to move—it was as hot and stifling as a tight scarf around my neck.

I passed by a basement that served as a study hall, a *beis midrash*, for the Ashkenazim, and I saw steps blackened with mildew leading down to it, and I heard some weak voices reading Torah in Ashkenazi tones and muttering querulously and complainingly in the holy tongue, as if they were so caught up in their daily troubles and their struggle to survive that all they desired was to receive better things from on high: a favorable marriage match, a good income . . .

And what of good deeds? If no holiness comes from heaven above, and there is no strength to move mountains in prayer, then perhaps it will be the good deeds that tip the scales.

As soon as I could, I questioned the widow's daughter, Sheindel, and learned that they sent people abroad to collect money for the poor, but the money was diverted to the more established members of the

Sephardic community. Chaya-Rivke, who herself was Ashkenazi, managed to receive very little, the barest minimum of assistance, after she had begged them and prostrated herself at the entrance to the Sephardic yeshiva, shouting, "*Gevald!* Help me!" Sheindel told me that since that outburst her brothers had been fortunately accepted to the Sephardic yeshiva, and were now studying there. But they were not allowed to feel at home, and were constantly afraid of being sent away. "If only they would find me a Sephardic man, then perhaps I could wed like the wealthy," she confided to me, her eyes sparkling.

So that's how it is, those who are rich have money and those who are poor only get more impoverished—so how will the world be set to rights?

One day my legs carried me out beyond the city's eastern walls, and I saw a splendid gate with two arches blocked with stones. I recalled things I had heard and realized I was facing the locked Gate of Mercy. Mounds of garbage were piled up around it, and inside those mounds, dogs and cats burrowed—even some mangy-looking children. They scratched themselves, jostling one another, and when they spotted me, their eyes burned with fear. I lowered my gaze and I prayed for the poor boys of the world. Not only did they have nothing to eat, but they were also deprived of Torah learning. I seated myself between two large stones, not far from all the refuse, and I fixed my gaze on the Gate of Mercy. Prayer was required, and good deeds were required, and I would offer both. In my heart a tempest was raging, and that tempest would turn my poverty into riches.

On my first Rosh Hashanah eve in Jerusalem, I sat at the table of the widow Chaya-Rivke, her daughter Sheindel, and her young sons Zechariah and Benjamin. The three oldest boys stayed in their yeshiva for the holy days. Zechariah was ten years old—a sickly youth, short-sighted, stuttering—and it was he who made the blessing over the bread. When he was about to make the blessing over the head of the fish, *May it be Thy will that we be the head and not the tail,* the words stuck in his throat and would not come out. He stared at the dish in front of him, aghast.

I looked at the fat fish, adorned with slices of carrot, and felt regret that it had not been blessed. And then I had an idea. I slid the wine for the benediction over to Zechariah. It was still almost full, and I told him to drink it all. He glanced at his mother apprehensively, blinking, and then with one deep gulp, emptied the glass. All of us looked at him, for his face had become flushed and all his hair stood up in ecstasy, as if on fire. In a clear, powerful voice he recited the blessing, took a piece of the fish, and put it in his mouth.

I have no idea what kind of soul was in the fish, but that evening, Zechariah was quite different from his usual self, and after he had sated his hunger, he opened his mouth and began speaking words of Torah. We listened to him quietly, drunk on his words. Sheindel brought him some sweets, and Zechariah ate and spoke.

Toward midnight he said the Grace-after-the-Meal blessings, then his head slumped onto the white tablecloth and he fell asleep. The other boy, Benjamin, also fell asleep at the table. The flames of the dying oil lamps danced as they drew in the last drops of oil. The faces of my own distant little boys rose up in front of my eyes. Pain filled my chest as if a bird's wings beat against my ribs. Chaya-Rivke smiled at me with a bashfulness that I had never seen in her before. She winked and whispered in a warm, yet stifled voice, "Who knows, Gittel, perhaps you are the gold coin that God sent me hidden inside the mouth of the fish that we serve on the High Holy Days . . ."

But the simple Chaya-Rivke forgot that gold is too rich for a person used to eating only fish. And when Zechariah's moment of glory passed, he walked about silent and downcast, as if he found it difficult to return to ordinary life.

Toward the end of the Festival of Tabernacles, he complained of a headache. His mother laid him down to rest in a darkened room and placed damp cloths on his forehead, but his temperature began to rise. Thirst made his lips crack and set his face aflame. Chaya-Rivke brought a holy man to recite psalms. He sat in the doorway of the room, muttering and sighing for days on end, but Zechariah's fever continued to soar.

The autumnal month of Marcheshvan arrived, and with it, a heavy easterly wind. The windows were always kept shut, and the air in the house grew more stagnant than ever. Chaya-Rivke and Sheindel never moved from Zechariah's bed. I cooked and washed and ironed. The acrid scent of camphor was everywhere. The house was sunk in silence, and when we spoke among ourselves, it was in whispers. The only sounds were the droning psalms and, when the man went home to rest, the ticking of the clock.

I was familiar with this mumbling, ticking silence. Three times in the course of my life I had heard the footsteps of the Angel of Death, and twice he took away the soul that he had come for.

I prayed for Zechariah as I had for those others, but this time, I did not give myself over to sorrow and dread. My soul drove me to venture beyond the city walls, and every day toward sunset, my legs would carry me down the paths to the south and east. I breathed in the scorched air that cried out for a drop of water, and—between the heaps of stones on which thistles grew, between the olive trees and the dusty carob trees—the buds of a new love stirred in my heart. I listened to the sounds around me and I heard the moans of the earth, the cries of the ever-restless wind trapped beneath the soles of my feet. I looked at the impoverished sheep in the Ishmaelite herds, at the shepherds who bend low to Allah, and felt pity for this hard, parched, impoverished land.

Yet the thought occurred to me that surely it was on account of this punishing clime that God had placed his ladder here. I felt as if a door were opening in me and, from inside it, there issued a hidden path, as narrow as a trail for goats. I thanked the Master of the Universe for His wisdom, again and again I asked Him to purify me of the dark spirit inside me, of the memories and the nightmares that disturbed my repose.

And when evening fell and I turned back to the city, I asked the heavenly court to take pity on Chaya-Rivke and her son Zechariah and not to separate them, unless for some higher purpose that we, in our lowliness, could not fathom.

At the end of the month of Marcheshvan, as he was sleeping, the soul of the child slipped from his body.

It happened at night. Chaya-Rivke was dozing on the sofa in the next room and I had taken her place next to his bed. Zechariah's sister Sheindel sat by his head, wiping the endless beads of sweat from his forehead. The psalm-sayer was sprawled on the floor, singing in a weary voice, his eyes closed. These are the hours when the angel steals away souls, and it's vital not to cease saying the prayers, not even for a moment.

Suddenly, I noticed that the man had ceased his mumbling. He opened wide his eyes and covered his mouth with his hand, staring at the oil lamp. A large black moth was fluttering around the flame.

Sheindel had dozed off, her hand resting on Zechariah's forehead. The psalm-sayer closed his eyes and resumed singing, but both he and I knew that the youth was gone. A heavy spirit descended upon me and I slept.

When I awoke, the moth had disappeared, and the psalm-sayer was dozing in his corner. Sheindel awoke as well, stroked Zechariah's forehead, and took fright. She embraced her brother and propped him up. I brought the oil lamp to his nose and we saw that the flame did not move.

Years before this, the great Maggid, Rabbi Dov Ber of Mezeritch, sat on his high-backed chaise longue overflowing with cushions, his lame left leg extended in front of him and covered with rabbit furs.

He wore white, as always, and his face was so pale that it was like the color of his clothes. Now the spirit whispered in his ear and revealed to him that his only son, Avraham, was about to die. The Maggid squeezed shut his eyes, and remained this way for a long time. When he opened them, he knew what had to be done to save his child. In a weakened but decisive voice, he ordered his attendant, Rabbi Feilet, to bring him two of the most influential men in the region.

When they appeared before him, he commanded them to travel to the city of Kremnitz and arrange a match between his son Avraham and the daughter of the illustrious Rabbi Meshulum Feivish Horowitz. "Bring her here with all possible haste!"

The emissaries filled a wagon with rolls of silk fabric and tailored suits, and they set out that same day.

When they arrived in Kremnitz, they were taken aback to discover that the holy congregation there had not even heard of the Maggid. The following morning, they loaded everything that they had brought with them onto the wagon and, with great noise, with the cracking of whips and with the chiming of bells, they traveled from the inn where they had spent the night to the home of my father, Meshulum Feivish Horowitz. Everyone came out to gaze at the lavish wagon. My mother also went out and saw it stop at the entrance of her house. Two distinguished men climbed down and addressed my mother. They remained standing before the steps, not entering the house out of modesty and respect. They spoke of their great rabbi, of his recently widowed son, and of the Maggid's wish to make a match between his son and her daughter.

My mother burst out laughing and said that I was only twelve years old, and it was a little early to seek out a groom for me.

But the emissaries continued to speak of the excellent match, and in the end, she shrugged and declared, "Well, I have a husband, thank God! Let him decide and do as he thinks best!"

My father was sitting, as he always did, in the house of study, and when they came to tell him that his wife was looking for him, he left his book open and returned home with a heavy heart. He invited the illustrious guests to enter, listened to them with some suspicion, and questioned them about how the Maggid lived, about the hours that he spent studying Torah, about his prayers, about his clothing, until he had no more questions.

My father hesitated, saying that his daughter was too young and completely unprepared for marriage. But the words of the emissaries spoke to his heart and, in the end, they convinced him. The two men took his hands and cried, "Mazel tov!"

In the course of the day during which my fate was sealed, I sat at my mother's market stall, and snatches of rumors reached my ears about the well-disposed emissaries from the north. All the market people knew that they were in our house and everyone whispered and winked at me, but I understood nothing. And when the day dipped toward evening, I skipped home between the puddles, a bag with the day's earnings in my hand. When I came to our street, I saw my mother waiting on the steps with tears in her eyes. Frightened, I ran to her and she hugged me. She led me to the back entrance, and when we came into the kitchen, she spread out her hands and whispered that the time had come for my match, that esteemed men had come all the way from Mezeritch in the north, and now my father and the emissaries were poring over the details of the marriage contract.

My mother opened the door a crack, and we sat at the kitchen table and listened to what was being said in the room. I heard the voice of the scribe, Chaim-Berel. He spoke my father's name with awe, and then he coughed, whispered with someone, and said the name of Rabbi Dov Ber, the great Maggid of Mezeritch. Even though I had never heard his name before this, I was moved as I waited for the name of the groom.

"His son, the illustrious rabbi, Rabbi Avraham, who has been widowed for a short while . . ."

I felt a chill go through my entire body. So he was no youth, but a rabbi! And how did his wife die? I pressed myself close to my mother, my head to her bosom. I didn't want to hear any more, but fresh voices, unfamiliar to me, rose from the room. The emissaries announced that they agreed in advance to all the conditions, and they had but one demand—that the wedding take place immediately.

"But what's the haste?" my father wondered. "What of the customary twelve months to give the maiden time to prepare?"

At this, one of the emissaries replied to him in a decisive voice, "Those are the Maggid's orders." He would say no more.

There was silence on the other side of the door. My heart beat wildly and I thought, *So my father must call it off.* And at that moment, my mother jumped up and stormed into the room. "Have you ever heard of such a thing? How are we to prepare the bride's trousseau?"

The emissaries remained calm. They promised that they would take care of everything and they soothed my parents with great patience. The nuptial contract was written immediately, clause after clause. I let my head drop and burst into bitter tears. When my mother returned to the kitchen to bring out more brandy, I raised my head and saw a large wet stain in the middle of the tablecloth.

A few days later, I was sitting with my mother on a wagon that the rabbi's men had hired. It was decked in a white fabric and adorned with green boughs. The driver gazed in wonder at the many women who came to say good-bye to me. They handed my mother cakes and pies, and with downcast eyes, they muttered blessings for fertility and placed small gifts wrapped in ribbons in my lap.

It was early in the morning. A splendid blue headdress sparkled on my mother's head. She was wearing a new blue dress and had a festive white pinafore fastened about her waist. I had never seen her so jubilant as on that morning. Her fingers caressed the sable fur the emissaries had given her; she chewed luxurious almonds and raisins and spoke incessantly about how I had been blessed with an excellent match.

But I felt that, in her heart, she was not with me. For the first time in her life, she had set out on a long journey, and she was elated to be seeing the world and its wonders. Her large body took up space on the seat next to me, and a sigh of pure pleasure escaped her lips. I held my breath, held in my tears, raised my eyes to the window of the second floor of our house, and searched for my father there.

Wasn't he even going to wave good-bye?

Father would not be coming to Mezeritch for my wedding so as not to waste time that should be spent studying the Torah. *How much can someone love the Torah?* I thought. My stomach churned with sorrow and disappointment. Even Chaike the matchmaker, who was surely angry at having lost a client, even she had come to catch a final glimpse of me with her squint eye.

So what of my father? Was he not still my father? And had I not been, till now, his beloved daughter?

He must simply be hesitating, I'd thought, his eyes on his sacred books, but his heart on the momentous event happening here, beneath his window.

The rabbi's men pulled up in a wagon decked out with bells. They touched the round brims of their black hats and smiled at us with satisfaction. Then they reached down from the wagon and shook hands with all the townsfolk.

"And the honorable rabbi and the girl's father, where might he be?" the emissaries wondered.

"Studying in his room," they were told.

The two exchanged confused glances, but then decided that there could be no further delay. One of them called out loudly, "Well then, we must set out! May good fortune be with us!"

Their wagon driver cracked a whip over the backs of his horses, and ours followed him. The crowd that had gathered scattered to either side and someone shouted, "Make way for the bride!"

I turned back and finally saw my father standing at the window, pressing his white palms to the glass. His face looked blurred through my tears. And so I recall him now, pale and blurry, locked away with his sacred books as if imprisoned in a tower.

I was lonely on that journey and even lonelier because I did not travel alone.

It was a very clear day. A soft winter sun caressed the beech trees, streams and puddles sparkled like mirrors. From afar, the blond hair of the Ruthenian peasants looked like golden helmets. Expanses of green meadows spread out at the sides of the road, covered with grazing horses and pigs. Geese scrambled between the puddles, sending up sprays of water, and a great flock of birds drifted high above. Herons perched in the trees, their white wings spread out like wet laundry.

Barefooted peasant children ran behind the wagon, their blue eyes wide as they stared at me like some kind of doll. I really did look like one, wearing a pink silk dress and a pink dress coat, my hair swept back in a ribbon that looked like a butterfly.

My mother sat up straight. By turns, she would look fixedly at the book and then raise her eyes, drawn to the vistas that spread out before us, struggling to be a pious woman whose every fiber was intent upon prayer. Each time she looked around, her mouth would fall open in wonder, and when she went back to the book, her mouth would purse again and her face grew stern.

Perhaps my father is right, perhaps I'm too young to marry. I looked sideways at my mother and couldn't understand how she could have agreed to such a hasty wedding, and with a groom she had never seen. It made no sense, yet it was really happening. What would come from all this? Should I stop the wagon, run home to my father, and plead with him to consult his books, reflect more on the matter? And who was this man, the Maggid, whose wishes were carried out with alacrity by two respectable men such as these? And his son . . . I closed my eyes tight and asked God to show me the face of my future husband.

I was a child, a frightened child.

The children who wandered in the fields looked happy enough to me, even the horses and the pigs seemed content, as did the geese and the birds. They were living their lives as usual, the life they were used to, and it was only for me that everything had changed.

It was in honor of this change that they had sewn me a pink dress, that a wagon had been hired for me and decked out in white. From time to time, my mother would steal glances at me from the corner of her eye, and when I looked back, she would evade my gaze.

My fingers stroked her arm and, to my surprise, she caught hold of my hand and held it tight. She didn't turn to face me, but her lips quivered and the prayer book fell into her lap.

"*Meine Tochter,* my darling daughter," she muttered.

I moved close and pressed against her sturdy body. My mother embraced me and encircled my head in her arms, for a long time, I curled up in her lap like a babe in a cradle.

The afternoon sunlight had already weakened when we crested a hill and entered the broad expanse where the city of Rovno lies. My mother adjusted her headdress, drew herself up, and said that she just knew—it was something in the air—that many Jews lived here.

But as we galloped forward, mud spraying to both sides, the first thing that I noticed was the birds. Large and small birds of all hues were wading in the shallow marshes left by the rains, flapping and shrieking raucously. Clouds sailed through the sky, growing heavier and heavier. The shadows cast by the clouds mingled with the shadows of birds circling overhead until the entire landscape seemed somber and strange, lurching between light and shade.

I sat frozen in place, my heart beating wildly.

My mother felt none of this. Again she opened her handkerchief filled with raisins, and then her eyes curiously sought out the Jews whom she had no doubt lived in this area.

And then we saw them. In groups of just one or two at first, dressed in Jewish clothes and wearing boots, they rushed out of the courtyards of farmhouses and greeted us in broken Yiddish. Then we passed small towns, and swarms of children with sidelocks ran to us with cries of "A wedding!" and "Look at the bride!" When they reached the wagon, they fell silent.

After the children, mothers came out of the houses and stood at a distance with their daughters, pointing excitedly to me and shaking their scarf-covered heads.

The closer we got to Rovno, the greater the number of Jews we encountered, and the more daring the women. Some of them even came up to us and felt the silk of my dress.

It was only when we entered the city itself that I began to have a sense of my future father-in-law's stature. A crowd of men and women surrounded the wagons. The men, who were wrapped in black gowns, pressed around the rabbi's emissaries, shaking their hands and making all kinds of requests. The women and the children swooped down on my mother and me, buzzing around us like bees, blessing us, raising their hands in the air, asking me to touch them. When I did so, tears sprang from their eyes.

The final leg of the journey felt like a dream, with people lined up along the sides of the road to bless us and to praise the name of the Maggid. Along the entire length of the journey people were waiting for us by the sides of the road to bless us and to praise the name of the Maggid. Women and young girls in white dresses opened wide their arms to me and asked me to bestow upon them a small portion of my good fortune.

My mother's sadness changed back to joy. She sat up as straight as a queen, the blue headdress hoisted like a crown on her head, her eyes shining. From time to time, she wiped the sweat from her face with a handkerchief, breathed in deeply, and in a choked voice, said to me, "Gittel, I simply can't believe the great honor that has befallen you!"

Smiling demurely, I tried to evade the women's fingers, their sweaty hands, their smiles and their jealousy. I was pushed into the corner of the wagon, squeezed there like a fish in a net. But a bridegroom awaited me at the end of this wondrous journey . . . *What kind of man will my husband be?* I wanted to shout. They went on standing by the sides of the road, excited and elated, and not one of them could hear what was in my heart.

When we reached the first houses of Mezeritch, the sun was slowly setting, and a rosy golden light was descending on the world. The light fell upon our shoulders, as soft as gold dust. The birds hid among the boughs of the trees and the quiet of evening fell all around.

We were all tired. The horses dragged their legs, the wagon drivers made clicking sounds as they shook their heads from side to side to keep awake. The road led through a large, flat field of low grass, and at the end of the field, small wooden huts could be seen. My mother went on sitting upright, looking festive, but with her eyes closed, and I, on the other hand, had my eyes open and my body slumped backward. With a vacant, sleepy gaze, I stared at the sky, and suddenly I heard a sound like flowing water, like a whisper. I sat upright in my seat and rubbed my eyes. The whole of Mezeritch seemed to be coming toward us, hundreds of men, women, and children tramping through the grass. Splendidly dressed men in their Sabbath best, with women in white dresses and white headscarves, surrounded by a swell of well-washed and festively dressed children.

My mother looked at me in wonder. "Can all this be in our honor?" The horses slowed down and then, thinking better of it, dragged the wagons into the field to graze. In the light of the sunset, the field glowed as if it were on fire.

We sat in the wagon and waited. It was like watching a river overflow its banks, the water getting closer and closer. The women surrounded us like a white-capped wave. They did not shout, and did not try to grab my hands; they asked nothing of me, just looked at me with soft, gleaming eyes.

I felt a wave of dizziness. Was I riding upon a river of stars? Upon the frothy peaks of the waves? Were they spirits who had clothed themselves in the bodies of women, and if I tried to touch them, would I feel the transparency of water? Who were they? What did they want with me? My head was spinning and my body swaying from side to side.

I heard a shout go up around me, growing distant. Exhaustion came over me, and a soft, heavy screen descended upon my eyes.

When I awoke, the sounds of whispers reached my ears: "What happened to her?" "She's only a child!" "As pink as a princess, what else can you say!" "Look, she's opened her eyes!" "Thank God, she's coming around!"

Smelling salts had been thrust under my nose, and my mother was bent over me. Behind her, there were excited women smiling, murmuring, and sighing. They propped me back up.

The murmuring of women hung in the air. My head was still spinning and I could barely stay seated, and yet I smiled at them apologetically for having caused such alarm. I smoothed my dress and folded my hands. The women followed my movements closely and I saw a change in their eyes, the concern replaced by something different, something that glowed and sparkled.

My mother asked if I was all right. I laughed and a wave of laughter rose from those around me, like an echo. I drew myself up, and my eyes gazed above their heads.

The two emissaries got down from their wagon and the entire large black gathering of men moved away from us and stood to recite the evening prayers. For the first time in my life, I saw the power and the beauty of prayer outside in the fields. They stood with their faces turned to the east, and I could see their profiles as they prayed. Their eyes were shut, their beards lit up with the fading hues of the sun, and their reverent gestures clearly visible against the vast, flat field of green grass tinged with gold.

They detached themselves from the world, their spirits transported to a distant and lofty place, and in that moment, I was reminded of wild geese in flight. I felt the blood flowing in my veins, I was seized by wonder, and suddenly it was clear to me that it had indeed been good fortune that had brought me here.

Two days later, at exactly the same time of evening, my mother brought me to a small room, closing the door as she left, and there I met my husband-to-be. He was standing in a corner, his back to the doorway, and he did not turn around to look at me. I was wearing a gorgeous dress made entirely of lace, and my head, which was now shaved and bare and smooth, was adorned with a white headdress.

My starry headdress, I thought, touching the delicate embroidery. *And here I am, for the first time, together with my bridegroom, the two of us alone in a room without windows, and he does not look at me.* A slight shiver ran down the nape of his neck, as if he were weeping or praying, or perhaps he was cold.

I made no sound, I did not take a seat on the sofa off to the side, I remained standing next to the door, standing very straight and biting my lip. I did not want to be afraid of the tall gaunt man who had turned his back to me, who in a very short while would acquire me with a ring. I wanted to come up close to him and to tell him that I was his bride, Gittel, but fear crept into my heart. I was just a little girl, and so what happened was that I began to cry.

The tears that coursed down my cheeks were silent, yet he sensed them and turned to face me. I stopped crying, I felt the blood drain from my face and knew I was very pale. Rabbi Avraham, my bride-groom, tried to smile, but his eyes remained almost completely closed.

The room was dim, and a lantern spread a faint and watery light, which tinted his twitching eyelashes with a yellowish hue. The smile, which resembled a grimace, sat suspended on his lips, limp and mirth-less. It passed through my mind that he looked like the people who fulfill the tradition of getting drunk on the festival of Purim, and without intending it, I rubbed my eyes and laughed up at him.

He was much taller than me, a little stooped, his face long and swarthy. His beard was soft and curly, the color of cinnamon. His eyes deterred me. They seemed to peer at me out of the mist of a dream. But his crooked lips were soft and ruddy, and despite his silence, his face spoke to me. I gathered up my courage and went to sit on the sofa. I arranged the dress all around me and waited for him to say something. He went on standing in the farthest corner, locked in his silence.

O, my husband! O, Rabbi Avraham! cried a voice in my head.

And that was how, in fearful silence, I met my future husband.

When the door was opened again, the tumult of the outside world rushed in. My mother hugged me, and some young men surrounded Rabbi Avraham. Shouting "Mazel tov!" and singing "How to Dance before the Bride," they brought us to the wedding canopy.

Everything was prepared for the ceremony, and yet we were delayed all the same.

"The Maggid is closeted in his room," someone whispered in my ear, her eyes rolling upward to invoke higher powers.

A white veil, almost transparent, hid my face and no one could see how pale I was. My mother was anxiously wiping perspiration from her forehead. A large crowd of women milled around behind me, and there was an even larger crowd of men, most of them wearing round fur hats. They filled the benches that were set out around three sides of the wedding canopy.

The sound of low voices, relaying secrets and whispering, filled the air and buzzed in my ears. "Like a living doll . . . an angel . . . the Rebbe knows . . . who knows that . . . hush, shush . . ."

Suddenly, all the voices fell silent and it was as if everyone sighed together with sheer amazement.

I stood on tiptoe and craned my neck, but was too short and could see nothing. I blinked angrily beneath the veil, and then I saw him pass like a flashing sword. My father-in-law approached us limping, and an azure light, like that of the morning star, radiated from his eyes and forehead.

Could that be the Maggid? I was amazed. Short and weak? Dragging his left leg? Why was he wearing a white robe as if it were Yom Kippur, the Day of Atonement? And how he looked at me! Could he see inside me? My body started to squirm. I placed one of my hands firmly upon my belly and, with all the strength I could muster, restrained myself from breaking into a scream.

The Maggid hastened his steps, leaning his right arm on the man at his side, and dragged his infirm leg with small but rapid movements. At last, he stopped opposite me, his head only a little higher than mine, and without saying a word, opened one of his palms in front of my covered face. A tremor went through the fine fabric, as if a breeze had blown across it, and my body began to relax. Then he laid his hand on my head, lightly and carefully. The blue light flowed toward me and I lowered my gaze. He whispered, *"Maydele"* so softly that only I could hear. And from that moment, I was entirely his. I wanted nothing else, nothing but to feel his affection.

But my groom, Rabbi Avraham, confused me. His almost-closed eyes were distant and wrapped in meditation, and when they asked him to say the blessing over the goblet of wine, he froze for an instant and an expression of repugnance passed over his face. I looked at him attentively. Despite my youth, I comported myself gravely, and whenever I felt a moment of weakness, my eyes searched out the Maggid. Only he sees me, I'd thought, only he knows how my face went ashen as I felt another presence make an entrance. The Angel of Death had arrived. He was clothed in white, and was standing like an attendant under the wedding canopy. Had he come for me? For Rabbi Avraham? Why wasn't the Maggid calling out that the ceremony must be stopped, suspended immediately on account of the immense present danger?

My mother, on the other hand, was brimming with happiness. She stayed in Mezeritch for all the days of hosting and feasting by the most important townsfolk. In the chamber where we were sitting, she made sure to hear what was said around the men's table and everything moved her to tears. She did not so much walk, but rather skipped or floated about, decked out like a peacock at all hours of the day, eating incessantly. Anything that was served, she ate with great relish, and between one meal and another, stuffed herself on almonds, raisins, apples, and various sweets.

At night, we lay huddled in one bed. Sometimes I awoke to find her sitting in the dark, among the pillows, munching on something. On her last night in Mezeritch, she did not let me sleep, but ate and spoke, recalled all the festivities that were held in our honor, all the speeches that were given, the splendor and glory of the wedding, the size of the house and the merits of my father-in-law, who made even the substantial men of the town look like children beside him. "You married into greatness!" she declared, embracing me out of sheer amazement.

I breathed in the scent of my mother, her large limbs, her soft breasts, the dishes she had eaten, and I buried my head in her lap and said, "I want to go home."

"Hush, hush . . ." She stroked my shorn head. "It is the Master of the Universe who brings couples together. And a Jewish daughter, well . . . at her wedding, she becomes a queen." Her body trembled around me as if the earth were shaking.

In a low voice, she told me that she'd heard all kinds of things in the marketplace, for example, about the peasant women who use herbs to rid themselves of the impurity in their bellies. Then they go down to the river and in the chill waters, they give birth to those impurities, and how rarely the child who is born remains alive and rises up and floats upon the water. How they leave it at the entrance to the church. "That baby is a child of God," the peasant women whisper, crossing themselves. But they do not speak about the babies that sink, only saying how, in the dark of night, screams and wails and cries rise from the water, as if a herd of pigs were drowning.

"The peasant women are wicked animals," my mother sighed, "but all the same, they are so wretched, almost barbaric . . . you can't help but pity them . . ."

I started to groan, to plead with her not to leave me here alone.

"Are you even listening to me?" she railed. "I only told you those things to show that our way is not like theirs. The Torah fills our hands with work, so we have no leisure for the lusts of the flesh."

Her lips quivered. She pushed me forward a little and, from under a pillow, pulled out a bag of raisins. She whispered, "The Jews you have married into are different from us. Their spirit is different . . . go with that spirit, my little Gittel."

"But my husband . . ."

"That's enough! You have been blessed with a good match, a family of Hasidim. As for complaints—*ouff*—they're from Satan!"

The next day, at dawn, she left Mezeritch. I stood at the window, like my father two weeks previously, and I watched her wagon disappear into the distance. It was cold in the room. I sat trembling on the bed for a long time before I finally stuck my head out of the door and cautiously sniffed around.

The house was quiet. I went to the kitchen, and there I found Froumeh the cook and her daughter Rivke roasting liver over the fire and frying onions. Froumeh ran to the samovar and poured me some tea, sat down in front of me, and gazed at me with her huge tired eyes.

I drank slowly and I fought back my tears. Rivke, who was around my age, smiled at me shyly and went back to working by the stove, flushed and sweating.

I turned away from her and stretched out my neck like a stork. Tears filled my eyes and almost overflowed. I wiped my face with a cloth that reeked of onion, then jumped up and fled.

I did my weeping inside a large closet full of pressed sheets. I lay on the white pile and I begged God to give me back my old life. *Please cancel the marriage, wipe away everything that has happened!* Sorrow covered me like a blanket, and slowly, very slowly, I fell asleep.

In my sleep, I saw myself standing naked on the shores of a quiet lake. Suddenly, a fat golden fish leapt from the water with a gurgling sound. I stretched out my hand, with a great longing to touch it, and tumbled face-first into the lake. The dark, freezing water was all around me. I thrashed at the water, shouting, "Help! *Gevald!*" As my mouth filled with water, I continued to scream. In the blink of an eye, I saw the fish leap up and disappear among the rays of the sun. I lay on the sand on my back, in the place where I had previously stood, and a deep, wordless voice, like the cooing of doves, was in my ear.

On awakening, some moments passed till I realized where I was: Mezeritch, in a closet, on a pile of sheets, alone. I picked myself up and gave thanks to the Holy-One-Blessed-Be-He for restoring my soul to me. But the voice from the dream continued to reverberate. Someone was standing outside the closet, speaking almost in a whisper, like someone talking to himself.

I pushed the door of the closet till it opened a crack and creaked on its hinge. There I discovered the Rebbe, my husband's father, sitting upright on a tall-backed chair. His fingers forcibly gripped the armrests and his eyes were closed. His pale lips, overgrown with the white hairs of his beard, murmured so gently and slowly that had I not heard him, I would not have thought he was speaking.

I slowly emerged from the closet. After I had slithered from the pile of sheets, with great caution, I placed one foot on the wooden floorboards. They creaked, so I froze and tried not to breathe. I waited for the beating of my heart to calm, and then slowly, slowly and warily, raised my right leg to take another step. It was like walking through a field of thorns, of snakes and scorpions. And that was how I moved toward the doorway, frozen in place and then creaking, frozen and then creaking again. The doorway was covered with a curtain, and on the way to it, I had to pass the Rebbe's chair. He continued sitting with closed eyes, sunken amid the high armrests, distant and mumbling.

When I got near him, I ceased breathing altogether and turned my face to the wooden floor. And then I felt his hand take hold of my dress. I looked at the thin white fingers, with the blue lines intertwined all along them, and I was filled with dread. I was caught. Like the golden fish in my dream, I wanted to slip away and escape, but my holy father-in-law had caught me in his net. I raised my eyes and I saw him leaning forward in his chair, almost falling off it in the effort to grab my dress. His mouth was open and his eyes sparkled with laughter. I straightened up and, with all the politeness I could muster, said, "Good morning, sir."

He winked and sat up, letting go of the dress. The soft checkered fabric fell back around my black-stockinged legs, and, though it was really hard for me, I spoke. I felt like the penitential goat being sent astray into the desert on the Day of Atonement and humbly sent forth my words into the room.

"Life is bitter for me, sir . . . I wander around the gloomy corners and recesses, which are the only quiet places in the house. All I want to do is to get away, but I don't know where I would go. Everyone is always busy, even my master's wife has no leisure. In my father's home, I became used to doing things . . . but here, they don't seem to need me even in the kitchen. And your son, well . . . my worthy husband, Rabbi Avraham . . . where is he?"

Since the week of the wedding, I had hardly seen my husband. Sometimes I caught a glimpse of his tall figure standing next to a window with a book in his hands. Then he would be standing with his back to me and facing toward the window, so immersed in what he was seeing that he didn't hear my footsteps. Once or twice, I retraced my steps; I trod on the floor harder with the heels of my shoes, but I could not draw his attention. He seemed downcast, as if about to fall straight into the window, and his narrow, lonely back stirred in me the desire to touch him.

His everyday *kapote* was sewn from a coarse fabric that was frayed at the shoulders. *My solitary husband,* I thought. *He's like that funny bird who pecks a hole in a tree and then sits inside that hole and peeks out.*

After he left, I'd go over to the place where he had been standing and look out through the glass. There were the black wooden houses of our Jewish neighbors, mud-covered geese and chickens in the back-yards. And far from the town, dipped in the bluish light of the horizon, a mountain reared up like the frozen wave suspended in the air as described in the story of the Exodus from Egypt.

To my mind, my husband must have been blind. Otherwise, why would he be avoiding me? Why did he not look at me and never smile even once? I did not yet know him, but I was already angry at him.

The truth was hidden beneath the anger, like demons in a closet, and there was the embarrassment and the silence of the first days of our marriage. But I was still a child, I still had daydreams of Queen Esther, and my husband's dark figure, frayed and stooped, fleeing down the corridors like a ghostly spirit, pierced my heart like a chisel.

I was frightened of him and I was frightened by the hatred that he aroused in me. At night, I buried myself under the feather quilts in the large bed where a trace of my mother's scent still lingered, and I consoled myself with visions of fury and revenge. Rabbi Avraham was a prince who came from the places of darkness; from his sunken cheeks and his eyes rose dark leaden vapors like those that hang over the marshes in the winter. A shiny black cloak fluttered behind him, and a black hood enveloped his head, casting a shadow over his face and his protruding ears. He was a prince of cold and mists from the region of death and he came to me from a room filled with evil spirits.

In my imagination, I waved my arms and with great effort, clapped my hands. My husband was affrighted and his knees buckled. I pushed him back into the room from which he had come; for an instant, the door opened and what I saw was utter darkness. The scent of mold filled my nostrils.

Afterward, it seemed to me that he really was gone, which made me very happy.

Another time, I saw him with the eyes of my soul as if he were made of dust. Even the sockets of his eyes had filled with dust. I took a broomstick and touched his navel with it, and my husband disintegrated into a cloud. And then, very slowly, the cloud dissipated.

And I saw other images like these, in all of them a kind of struggle, and in all of them, I vanquished my husband and I was happy about it.

Over the years that followed, I locked away my desire to vanquish him and take revenge. Only when I reached Jerusalem could I at last forget the wound to my heart, at last forget my humiliation and my anger, at last forget my body.

Yet on that long-ago day in a dim room of creaking floorboards, facing the question in my father-in-law's merry eyes, I was blazing with fury, sorrow, and humiliation.

"Patience, my daughter," I heard him say. "With patience everything will come, all in its proper time. Our existence in this world is only suffering and more suffering, and anyone who has much suffering must have patience . . ."

He looked upward, smiling, and I saw that two of his bottom teeth were missing. Here I was longing for my parents' home, and he was speaking to me, as if from a great distance, in praise of patience.

"It's like armor against the assaults of the world," he said. "It watches over our distress and does not allow us to fall into the darkness of exile."

I knew that by "us" he meant the Jewish people, I knew that for the time being we were here and could not see that we were the sons of kings, but the day would come when we would step out in azure and gold, floating lightly, on the path to redemption. But at that moment all I could think of was myself. I needed redemption, I was going into the darkness like a shadow, and it was not armor that I wanted but something else, soft as the duvet and the pillows piled high and filled with goose feathers. Like the scent my mother had left on the bed.

"This isn't my home!" I declared as my hands tightened to fists.

He was amused by me. I knew it by his smile. His eyes examined my face, interrogated me, looked inside my heart. And then he spoke to me in a low, melodious voice, describing my old home and my old life to me. As if he were there, in Kremnitz, as if actually in front of my house.

"It's made of dark wood," he said. "There are two floors, and the lower story is surrounded by a veranda with a railing. The windows looking out onto it are small with opaque glass. The yard is quite neglected, but at this time of year, it is full, brimming with all kinds of greenery, tall and short, all tangled up together. Flowers burst out of the wild growth, sending out tendrils to the railing, catching onto the wooden beams and turning the veranda into a flowering garden.

"Your young brother, almost a baby, who has been put down alone at the front door, thrusts his face in the petals of a blue flower. A bee emerges from the flower, buzzing around his nose, and he points at it and bursts out crying. The door opens and someone scolds him and wipes his face and goes back inside.

"Now the door stays open. A hen wanders up, squawking excitedly in front of the doorway, and a young peasant girl in a floral kerchief comes out of the house. She gathers up the hen in her arms and disappears to the far-off part of the veranda, the part that I cannot see.

"And your illustrious father sits on the second floor, under the gabled roof, from which a chimney rises. At the very top of the roof is a wrought iron rooster standing on one leg. Now I see him bending over one of the volumes of his sacred texts—the Talmud. He holds the tractate about the laws of damages and compensation. Standing before him is the leader of the Jewish community, his hat in his hands. The man who draws and carries water has fallen from a bridge that the leader of the community built over a channel. He broke a limb and now his wife is berating the leader.

"And the leader waves his hat and claims that the carpenter did shoddy work and so he should pay the injured water carrier from his own pocket. And what now, now I hear the sound of wailing . . .

"It's the water carrier's wife shouting brazenly, storming through the flowers, climbing onto the veranda, and stopping at the open door. She stands there and weeps.

"And the young peasant girl comes running back. She calls to the woman, 'Mistress Baiyla!' and ushers her inside."

I sighed loudly with yearning. With the confidence that this man could move and speak in dreams, I imagined going inside, into my father's house.

I closed my eyes and I told the holy Maggid about what went on in the women's part of the house.

"Leibush, my baby brother, is lying on a feather bed in a corner, sucking his thumb. My sister, Yocheved, is standing over a pile of clothes, folding and putting aside the ones to be ironed. Dasha, our servant girl, crosses the room with a flushed face, dragging her feet in their heavy peasants' shoes, her body tilted backward to balance the large rounded stomach of her first pregnancy. She's carrying a container full of apples to the storeroom outside. Soon, they will be made into jam or compote to eat after the cholent stew at the Sabbath meal.

"And my mother stands in the small kitchen, which is filled with the aromas of spices, a tin spoon in her hand and a stained towel tossed over her shoulder. She is stirring the buckwheat porridge as she prepares kasha. All the utensils are completely blackened by soot, as are the stones arranged around the opening for the fire. And the paraffin stove in the corner, the ceiling, the walls are all covered in soot.

"There is no window in the kitchen, and as my mother wipes the sweat from her face with a towel, she draws streaks of dirt and grease over it. With a long-handled poker, she stirs the hissing embers in the pail under the stove, puts pans on the fire, slathers them with goose fat, and when the grease is hot, pours the porridge over it. She pats it down with the underside of the spoon so that it'll be nice and flat and then covers it with a lid. Over that, she lays a heavy towel that will keep in the heat. And then she goes straight on to the dough, which has already risen, kneading it out and cutting it into quarters. At the center of each quarter, my mother places a mixture of potatoes and fried onions, and she takes hold of the corners of the square and folds them inward. Now the knishes are ready and she places them, one by one, onto the large frying pan.

"If this were a Thursday, then Dasha would be scraping the scales from a plump carp and pulling out its red entrails, the green gallbladder, and the white bladder sacs that we liked to hold and toss from hand to hand. She would be cutting the fish into slices and then giving them to my mother, who would stuff them and make them into gefilte fish for the Sabbath.

"On Thursdays, we would also prepare sweets for the coming Sabbath: the tagelach covered with a brown dusting of sugar, and the cookies made from carrots, sweet and pungent.

"And of course, that was the day we made dough for the challah—the Sabbath loaves—covering it with a flimsy cloth and leaving it till Friday morning.

"And at dawn the next day, in the pale light before sunrise, my mother would be braiding the dough, sinking nuts and raisins into it, and then coating it with a shiny layer of egg.

"And then, working quickly, she starts on the largest pot of all, the pot of cholent. She adds thick pieces of meat, peeled potatoes, chicken feet and thighs, rounded white bones dripping with grease, and beans the color of blood. She takes a length of beef intestine and stuffs it with a mixture of flour, meat, and potato, and then, with a needle and thread, she sews it up, tears the thread with her teeth, and places it deep inside the pot, which she then covers with a linen cloth.

"And now it's time for the generous chunks of fat, which will give the dish its taste. Then Dasha pours in water up to the top and puts in a bag with fresh eggs, and then my mother says, as she does every Friday, 'Let's hope that this comes out for Sabbath as nicely as it went in.'

"And she puts a lid on top, sealing it with a towel, and turns aside to wipe away the sweat dripping from her face and neck and staining her armpits.

"And now you run to the market, for the day before the Sabbath day is a good day for earning. And Dasha will clean and scrub the house and iron, and at noon, she will go out to the backyard and sit there, among the hens and the geese, with baby Leibush on her knees.

"And if Dasha's in the mood, she'll tell us stories about the gentiles in the village—beautiful and terrifying stories about them and their demons.

"When she speaks, her Yiddish is garbled with the language of the peasant women. And her kerchief is woven from black and red yarn. And her golden hair is in a long braid, slipping out of her kerchief. And when she laughs, her cheeks are round and flushed, and her blue eyes sparkle . . ."

And, as suddenly as I had begun to speak, I fell silent.

I could have told him about my father, and how he had taught me to read and write. The two of us would be leaning over a large sacred book, the black hair of his beard caressing the pages with their holy letters and sometimes touching my cheeks.

First, we studied Genesis, and then we studied the holy families: Abraham and Isaac and Jacob, their hearts like a garden of love for the Holy-One-Blessed-Be-He. He sends them words, dreams, angels, and they leave their homes for His sake, sleeping on stones for Him, ready to sacrifice their sons and even to grip the blade of a knife for Him.

By their sides are Sarah, Rebecca, Leah, and Rachel—faithful only to their sons, to their most beloved sons and no one else. And so the stories are spun of strands of loving-kindness and strife and contention. And my father touches the words with the hard end of a goose quill, and when I have a question, he lowers the feather to the bottom part of the page, reading the commentaries by scholars such as Rashi or Ibn Ezra. And he chants and his eyes are half-closed. And when we make progress in learning, he holds the feather and I read out loud. Not chanting as he does, but word for word so as to understand what is written. Sentence after sentence, with a pause after a few sentences, when he says, "Here a Jew sits and reflects upon what he has read."

But I drink in the words with a great thirst, and as for stopping to reflect—well, I can do that later. Our hours of study together are more precious than gold and I do not want to pause, I do not want to stop. And the candlelight dances like water on the pages, and my father and I stream across them like two ancient sailors. Above us, the firmament sparkles with stars. And around us the Children of Israel are multiplied, as countless as the sand upon the shores of the sea, and we are borne aloft toward the Holy Land.

Before us spread fields of wheat, vines that curl and twist, fig and olive trees. And the blazing sun picks out the ripe fruits. And a sweet, heavy juice flows from the pomegranates that have split like open mouths, from the soft figs, from the carobs hanging like black fingers on the trees. And the air that I breathe is no longer the fusty air of my father's study, but soft and clean, as if it came from the very mouth of the Holy-One-Blessed-Be-He.

In my imagination, I could see myself walking beside Abraham, Isaac, and Jacob, our holy forefathers, and their wives and children. All of them going over the hills and traversing the deserts of the Holy Land, and me with them. We wander, searching for water, for food. At night, we gaze at the stars just as Jacob did when he fled from Esau, and I feel part of this ancient family drama.

All the sweet hours I had spent in my father's company rushed through my mind as I stood there, facing my father-in-law, and like Lot's wife, I was seized by an immense desire to look back, to immerse myself forever in what had been and was no longer. What awoke me from that dream, what brought me back to my body? A cold wind swept around me, and for a moment, my eyes searched for an open window.

Fine, trilling sounds reached my ears, and I was surprised to see they issued from the Maggid's throat. He chirped like a bird and clucked his tongue, his arms fluttering in the air, and loudly clapped his hands a few times.

Then he fell silent, calm again. His arms returned to the chair's armrests, and his eyes looked at me searchingly but smilingly from beneath his heavy eyelids. A short while later, he said in his normal voice, "Sometimes God and Satan fight over the soul of a person, my daughter, and then it's good to play the fool, to behave like an idiot, and in this way, Satan is confounded."

After that day, things changed for me in my husband's home.

At dawn, I would take up my place in the kitchen, where Froumeh and her daughter Rivke walked around bleary eyed. They lived in a small windowless room next to the kitchen, sleeping together in a hard, narrow bed, and I got used to hearing them chattering and rapidly became close with Rivke. Both of us helped Froumeh with the cooking, and when there was no work, we would escape to their little room and lie on the bed, side by side. Opening our eyes wide in the thick dusk, we would speak about anything and everything that crossed our minds. She told me that, when she was a baby, her mother had become a widow and that the Maggid, out of the goodness of his heart, had brought them into his home, which was now her home, for she had no other.

Another thing she told me was that, when she was a very young girl, she thought the Maggid was her father. And she laughed about it and said that the thought had done her much good. "He used to sit me on his knees, and would give me a cube of sugar when I was sad, and when I stroked his beard and pulled his sidelocks, he would make the sounds of a horse neighing. And on his lap, I would gallop far away, away from the reach of Mother or the scolding of Mistress Sarah, of whom I was always afraid, and whom I fled whenever she came into the kitchen . . ."

Mistress Sarah was the Maggid's wife, a woman silent like no other, dressed all in black. I was also terrified of her. I stroked Rivke's arm that was always sweating under my fingers, and said that, if I weren't married, the two of us could go somewhere that was much, much better than here.

"Where, Gittel?" I heard her voice in the shadows.

"To Jerusalem, Rivke'leh. I already tried to go there once before . . ."

"And what happened?"

"It didn't work out," I answered, a lump in my throat. It was as if I had swallowed something and it had stayed stuck in my throat.

In my childhood, I left Kremnitz only once. I took my brother Mote'leh, who was two years younger than me, and together we set out walking to the Land of Israel. We walked toward the hills, in the same direction as the flocks of storks. I remember the moment in which we passed the last houses and stood on a green hill and, all of a sudden, huge distances opened before us.

Blue summer skies with white patches of cloud stretched over our heads. Green and yellow fields lay beneath our feet, and there was a quiet like we had never known, a quiet in which you can hear the birds chirping, the frogs croaking, the cattle lowing—that quiet was all around us and swallowed the sounds of the village we'd left behind. We looked happily at one another and scampered down to the valley below.

For hours, we walked inside beauty and within tranquility, imagining that we had reached paradise. We came upon a river flowing between apple trees, we paddled our feet in the water, and then we drank from it and ate apples. We followed along the banks of the river, enjoying the silvery glint of the fishes' bodies. Ducks sailed swiftly by, dipping their heads in the water and then surfacing with a screeching *gaa-gaa*. Everything was so beautiful that we had no doubt we were on the way to Jerusalem.

It was then we saw the goose. Solitary and plump, its white feathers shone in the hot sun. It was floating slowly, like a huge soap bubble, turning its head toward us and staring at us with round black eyes. From the opposite bank, there was a sudden sound of branches snapping. The goose froze and its head turned like a screw. A big fat man with a red face burst out of the bushes, and after him, there came another. They were both holding long, thin, sharp switches in their hands. The goose fluttered and propelled itself forward with clumsy movements. Its neck was outstretched and its eyes bulged from their sockets. The red-faced man and his friend chased after the goose, beating their switches on the mud at the edges of the river. The goose gathered speed, its body lurching from side to side and sharp, high groans burst from its throat. I shouted to my brother, "Run!" and we made a break for the trees behind us. We continued to run as fast as we could, as far as possible from that river, until both of us fell to the ground and my brother burst into tears.

"I want to go home!" he wailed. And suddenly, he clutched his head in dread and said, "My *kippa* . . . it fell off!"

I stroked his head until I saw that he had fallen asleep. His face was trembling in his sleep and I could see the milk teeth peeping out of his mouth.

I lay on my back, next to my brother, in the heart of a field of hay, and a distress I had never known moved down from my throat and filled my stomach. A cold wave went through me. The sky was blue and the clouds that wafted over it were thin as handkerchiefs. The sun was as warm as before, and yet I felt I was freezing. Wispy thoughts, translucent like those clouds, passed through my mind.

A woman cannot always know what she is thinking of, even when she knows she has glimpsed something important. And that's what I realized then, that something deep and unclear, dark and threatening, had been revealed to me and I was totally powerless to run away from it.

How long I lay there, screaming without letting out a sound, I do not know. All of a sudden, I heard dogs barking, the sky was gray, and the light had become pink and hazy. The barking grew louder. My brother woke up and burst into tears again. Only when the dogs reached us did I stand up and start shouting, "*Gevald!* Help!"

My brother pressed himself to my legs and buried his face in my knees. Large dogs surrounded us, baring yellow teeth and sniffing the air with quivering nostrils. Then a pack of villagers arrived. They drove away the dogs and stood gazing at us. They crossed themselves and laughed, speaking a strange language, and I kept silent and looked down. And then one of the men, who seemed to me like the leader of the pack, began to talk in Yiddish.

He spoke a strange Yiddish, guttural and all broken up into bits. A strange acrid smell wafted from his mouth as he spoke, and his rubber boots kicked the ground, scattering clumps of hay. But all the same, I was glad he was there and I answered him readily. I told him that we were from Kremnitz, me and my brother, and that we were on our way to Jerusalem. He scratched his head and told the others and everyone laughed.

An old woman with blue eyes detached herself from the group, pointed to the sky, and said something with great force. The man translated, "She says the real Jerusalem is up there. So where are you going? You'd better return home!"

They took us with them to the house of the leader. A one-room hut, foul and stinking. The women let us sit beside the oven, gave us bowls of diluted beetroot soup and a hunk of black bread. We ate the sour soup and fell asleep curled up at the foot of the stove.

We stayed in the village the following day among vulgar and dirty but hospitable people. When dawn broke, they opened the door to the yard and the smells of geese, pigs, roosters, and cows filled my nostrils. A swarm of barefoot children with shaven heads burst from the houses, and we stood in the yard confused, our feet sinking into the sticky mud.

My brother covered his eyes not to see the pinkish sacrilegious pigs and said to me, "Gitte'leh, what have we done? Let's pray to God!"

A wild spirit gripped me and, when I saw him so afraid, I stomped my feet in the mud and marched right into the herd of pigs. From that moment onward, I wandered among the animals in complete freedom, then left the yard and explored the high grass behind the hut. I hid under a tree whose branches were slender and curly, buried my head among the leaves, and pictured myself as the lost daughter of a king who had been found by the people of the forest. I pretended it was my fate to live among them forever, unknown.

I opened my mouth wide and shouted with sheer delight. Birds in the tree took flight in alarm, so I started to whistle to them and chirp between my teeth. And when the sounds of birds were around me again, I stood still and listened. A long time I spent under the tree of the birds, until hunger gnawed at my belly and drove me back to the hut.

Silent, I stood at the threshold. My brother was sitting on the ground, his eyes closed and his body swaying back and forth as if he were praying. When he heard my footsteps, he opened his eyes and looked shaken. Apart from him and the old woman, there was no one else in the hut. She came over and gave me bread and a thick slice of cheese. I slumped down beside my brother and mumbled the blessing over bread, then swallowed the food with large bites, almost without chewing, and the old woman laughed with her wide toothless mouth. Her black dress rustled. She stood over me and recited a string of unclear but ritualistic-sounding words, of which I understood only one: Jerusalem.

Excitement shook me, and I leapt up and ran back outside. I returned to the tree of the birds and, in some language that wasn't a language, I told them, I chirped to them, of the wonders awaiting me in the sky-blue city of Jerusalem.

∼

On our second night in the village, I had a dream.

An angel, with sidelocks and a beard, stood at the top of a tall palm tree. He spread his wide wings marked with eyes like the tail of a peacock and leapt down. I was standing beneath him, very close to the tree, and watched him falling toward me. His long black *kapote* blocked the light, throwing a growing shadow on my upturned face. I wanted to flee, but my blood froze in my veins and my legs were rooted to the ground. I saw his thin legs, their black leggings, emerging from the *kapote* fluttering under his wings, and I was seized by immense dread.

I awoke from my sleep sweating and confused. The room was not completely dark. Red embers darted in the black belly of the stove. Snores and whistles and sighs resounded in the air. For a moment, it seemed to me that I was in hell. Soon I calmed down and was able to move my limbs again. I shook off my sleep and stretched my legs.

It was so hot in the room that the fresh hay on which we were all lying had dried up and cracked. I still felt very excited, as if under the spell of some enchantment. The quiet and the heat, the sounds of the embers crackling, and the oppressive stench of the wooden walls—they wrapped around me and kept me safe from the evil forces running wild outside the hut.

Out there, the hunters stalked geese, dogs barked and ran around the tree of the birds, and from the top of the tree leapt a man who looked like a regular Jew, but with wings full of eyes and a bird's beak.

Until dawn, I stayed awake. The leader of the group was the first to rise and announced that he was going to fetch a wagon. I did not want to return to Kremnitz, and when we climbed up on the wagon and began to move, a prayer burst from my heart.

"Merciful God, Master of the Universe, why should I live like a sack filled with longing? Wave Your hand, the hand of Your wonders, for my sake. For the sake of Gittel, cause us to travel, but not to arrive. So that we never return to Kremnitz."

My first journey to Jerusalem came to an end with a blessing of thanks for my safe return in my father's synagogue, with new restrictions from my mother, and with the loss of my brother Mote'leh's love.

He was my sweet brother, my dear friend, and my confidant, who had hidden with me among the feather-down covers from our mother's large figure and thunderous voice. And in that white dusk, smelling of feathers, we'd decided to fight side by side when we were grown. Like Gog and Magog in the Bible, we saw ourselves conquering the kingdoms of Turkey and Russia and Poland, and opening the gates for the Messiah.

So I found myself alone. My brother did not call me a traitor, but I knew he scorned me for how I had behaved in the village. He no longer sought out my company, and when I tried to speak with him, he lowered his eyes and was silent.

His silence tortured me and made me seek his approval. I would walk behind him, pleading in a voice close to tears for him to speak to me again.

Sometimes I would catch him looking at me sideways, his eyes half-closed, as if seeing me from the bottom of a pit full of doubts. And to win him over, I took the blame for things he had done.

And so, I bore punishments that should have been for him: my mother hit me and I was forbidden to eat with the family. Worst of all, I was deprived of the time I loved so much, the hour my father would teach me reading and writing. I felt as lowly and scorned as a worm.

None of these things helped at all. I ate my meals alone in a corner of the kitchen, while he sat at the table, calm and smiling, and from time to time, threw me that same sideways glance.

In the end, I gave up and left him alone.

The utter loneliness after losing Mote'leh was one of the worst times in my childhood. More than six hundred Jewish families lived in our town. My father was a great scholar and my mother owned a stall in the market. Scholars and merchants came and went in our home. And yet I felt as if I were living in a desert.

At all hours of the day, I was subject to my mother's iron rule. I kept the home while she was at the market, and I took her place at the stall when she ran home to take care of anything urgent. The days were full for both of us, running back and forth. She rebuked me for being so slow, and she raised her arms to the heavens as she sighed, "What a block of wood you are! What a *goilem*! When will you grow up and become a real woman?"

But the truth was that I didn't want to be a "real woman," I didn't want to be like her, and when I caught myself behaving as she did, I would immediately do something that it would never have occurred to my mother to do—I gave bread to a beggar, I stroked the head of a child who tried to steal from our stall, I smiled at someone who came to buy and refused to accept her money.

Such frivolity earned me a strong tug on my earlobe, or my hair being pulled, two punishments of which my mother was particularly fond. It was because of this that my hair was sparse and weak, and my ears as soft and red as a cockscomb.

Once, when I was home alone, an old peasant woman came into our courtyard. She was known as a witch, and she stretched out her hands and felt my ears and offered me a healing potion for half a zloty. She held out a transparent vial in front of my face; it was filled with a red liquid, and she opened it and brought it close to my nose. A heady scent of flowers filled my nostrils. To pay her, I'd have to steal half a zloty from the pouch that my mother hid under the mattress.

I was seized by an immense desire to possess the bottle no matter what. I ran inside, my legs trembling, and I came back holding the money. "Here, it's yours. Be off with you!" I whispered and took the precious vial. She bit the coin, and then laughed cunningly and hid it away in her fist.

When she had gone, I went inside, sat, and looked at the vial. I took off the stopper and sniffed, poured a little onto my fingers, and rubbed my earlobes. A delicate, sweetish scent wafted to me. I poured another drop and rubbed it on my hair. In this way, drop by drop, I emptied the entire bottle.

My head was spinning with pleasure. I started to drift about the room with small dancing steps. I opened up the door of the wardrobe to see the mirror and looked at myself fondly. My dress whirled about me and my face was radiant with happiness.

Suddenly, I saw my mother standing by the door, watching me, shocked. I do not know how long she'd been standing there, but I have never forgotten the quiet of that moment. An expression of anger and repugnance distorted her features, her mouth hung open, and her nose sniffed the air. Without moving from the doorway, she held out her hand and pointed at the empty bottle, which was lying on the floor.

Then she blew past me on the way to the inner room. I heard her turning over the mattress, and then she shouted, "You little thief!" I went on standing in front of the mirror, my head bowed. She sat down in front of me and ordered in an icy, furious voice that I had never heard before, "Now you're going to clean the room so well, there'll be no smell at all!"

I scrubbed the floor and the walls, I polished the glassware and the silver and passed a duster over all the furniture and all the books, and when I had finished cleaning, she grimaced and said, "It still smells, clean it again!"

Three times I cleaned that room and everything inside it. Then she told me that I had to wash myself.

"Here?" I asked, shocked.

"Here!" she replied.

I dragged the large metal pail into the middle of the room. Then I heated the water and sat in it naked. I scrubbed my body, hair, and face with plain soap, and when I stood before her, washed clean and dressed in clean clothes, she rose and in an unyielding voice she ordered, "And now we'll go to the mikveh to clean your soul!"

At the ritual bathhouse, my mother lashed my back and neck with a bundle of twigs. I bit my lips and did not show how it hurt, and she went on beating me until she had no more strength. And then she let me go and gestured that I should enter the water.

I started to go down, one step at a time, swaying from side to side, and the cold water rose all round me. Water swirled round my back and covered it, reaching my shoulders. I walked farther along the descending slope of the ritual bath. The waters came up to my head, and slowly covered it. It was then I was gripped by panic. I tried to shout and my mouth filled up with water. I felt that I was choking, my body convulsing. And then I heard someone screaming outside the water. And then I lost myself.

When I returned to my senses, I was sitting on the wooden slats next to the mikveh, my naked body in my mother's arms.

Someone was slapping my back, and I was throwing up water and panting painfully. The mikveh lady was also bending over me, and her thick, strong fingers were massaging the nape of my neck. Then they wrapped me up in a blanket and laid me down on a bench. I closed my eyes and I did not open them until I realized I was lying in my bed.

But even then I could not rest. My throat was choked with anger and anger misted over my mind. For many days, I lay like this, under a pile of blankets, full of wretched thoughts. I thought about all the persecutors who had embittered my life, and first and foremost among them, my mother. Ranged behind her there was a small army of "real women"—Feigel, the rabbi's wife, pale and stingy; the slippery-tongued Dubeh-Dvoireh, wife of the ritual butcher; and Chaya-Leah, the woman who sold roosters and baby chicks. They and their maiden daughters, who resembled them in every way.

To punish this army of women, I wanted to die. I refused to eat or to drink, and when these women tried to feed me forcibly, I vomited into their hands and screamed, "You blood-sucking leeches! You horrible creatures! I hate you all!"

And so I drove them away and was left alone.

They fought back by ceasing to care for me. I lay between sheets that were no longer changed; I had sores and my tongue was swollen and dry. For several days, I was less a person than an animal left to die, lying in its own vomit. Who knows how all this would have ended, had not my father, my beloved father, suddenly descended from the world of his sacred books and religious rulings. He sat down by the side of my bed and looked at me with his sad, wise eyes.

My father did not speak, only looked at me, but from the moment that he entered, the world seemed to grow larger. I turned over on my side and pulled the rumpled sheets over my head. My father leaned over and laid his hand on my head. His hand was so gentle that it felt as light as a small bird. I hid my face in the pillow and asked him, "If I start eating again, can we go back to learning together?"

I looked up at him and saw his face stiffen. "Ask your mother's forgiveness, and then we can go back to studying . . ."

I beat my fist against my forehead. "But *Tateh*, that's not fair!"

He got up and pronounced drily, "If you will not respect your mother, and if you do not keep the commandment not to steal, we cannot study together."

Then he walked out.

～

It was hard for me to swallow my pride, but eventually, I got out of bed and asked my mother's pardon. After that, the two of us went to the homes of Feigel the rabbi's wife, Dubeh-Dvoireh the butcher's wife, and Chaya-Leah the rooster lady. I had to ask pardon and forgiveness from each of them. My mother whispered in their ears that people with a great spirit also have great passions.

And I sat abjectly, my fingers tugging at clumps of my hair close to my head.

My saintly father had always derided dreams, called them drops of burning oil from the cauldron of hell where limbs of the wicked were roasted. Of course this saddened me, for I loved my dreams, but I learned to keep them to myself, rolling them around my mind like small, secret marbles, until they became transparent and clear to me.

And now, a short time after the wedding ceremony, after the tears I shed in the closet and the long talk I had with my husband's father, a large gathering of venerable elders came to me in a dream.

They were sitting in two long rows in the arched shape of the letter *chet*, ח, in a spacious and empty vestibule. I had come in carelessly, quickly, as if on the way to somewhere else. And when I saw where I was, I stopped short.

They looked at me, all of them with their gray and white beards, all of them dressed in radiant white robes. And I was the only one standing in front of them, in a simple gray housedress with my hands thrust deep into my pockets. I felt my face redden, my hands restless as small animals in my pockets. One of them began to speak in a deep, resonant voice.

"We wish to take your husband, Rabbi Avraham," said the man. "There is no room for him where you are, and here he has a chair." He tilted his head and his eyes indicated Avraham's seat. I looked at the chair, empty like an open wound, and a shout escaped from me. My shout bounced around the chamber and splintered into echoes.

The chamber was lit with large candles on pedestals, and behind the illuminated part—where the old men sat—there extended an area of deep shadow I could not see the end of. One of the men rose with difficulty, leaning on his stick, and looked long and hard at me. When he started to speak, his voice quivered, and a cloud of dust bloomed from his throat, as if he hadn't spoken for years.

"The soul of your husband, my daughter, is one of the highest and the lightest. Lighter than a feather it will rise up, dragging the body after it like a lead weight. Have pity on it and free it from the travails of the flesh. Let his soul bloom, let it rise up to its origins and disappear in flight. Think of the plight of a bird that is tethered to a bough. Think of the plight of a bird. Think of a root that takes flight . . ."

Although my husband was nicknamed the Angel, he did not behave like one. He was an unusual person, incorporeal, almost haunted by the spiritual visions that gave him no rest. But he was the husband that I had been given, and to defend him was to defend myself. I felt as if I had taken a blow to my stomach, the way my breath caught and then burst out again, red as fire. I spat out burning words, directing them at the shadowy part of the chamber behind the old men, for it was easier for me to speak to that faceless darkness. How long I spoke I do not know, only that the slightest tinge of white began to seep into the chamber.

Then the old man with the stick lifted his free hand and cut me off. The faces of the old men grew pale until they were as white as the robes that they wore. The flames of the candles also waned. The whole place slowly faded like fabric left in the sun, and I awoke from the dream.

I lay sweating in my bed, and I tried to remember what I had said to the elders. But I remembered nothing.

And the following night, the dream recurred.

Again the elders sat in front of me. Again the flames of the candles, and I stood and spoke and shouted. And again the white seeped into the room and the faces faded. In the end, I lay in my bed, very tired, with no memory of what I had said.

And on the third night, everything happened like on the previous nights, only this time the old man got up and waved his stick in the air. His body swayed from side to side until he almost fell. I looked at the shiny floor, with its webbed veins like blue marble, and I heard his dusty voice speaking.

He said that they were giving me my husband as a gift for another twelve years. That's just what he said: "As a gift for another twelve years." Then I started to shout and did not stop shouting. The dream began with me shouting and ended with me shouting. Apart from that, I remembered nothing. I buried my face in the pillow and the image of my husband rose before me, only instead of arms, he had wings.

My birdlike husband went on living and keeping silent and evading me and his father. He continued to escape outdoors, to fields and rivers, and I after him, like a shadow. In the early years, I went out to bring him home, but later, I no longer went out for his sake, but for mine.

I was barely twelve years old when I dreamed that dream, and I slept alone in a room that was just mine. At the end of the corridor from my room was his, and sometimes, during the night, sounds would come from it like the growling of a large animal. I would cover my ears with a pillow and cry.

It has been years since I've wept tears. Tears are an ornament to sorrow, and I have detached myself from any form of ornament. Now sorrow has become a cavern that fills up my body. And in the morning, when I rise, I grope my way with aging hands, which are growing more and more mottled with brown spots. Sometimes, my hands get confused and believe they are young. Then the fingers leap, as light as butterflies, and on those days, I can heal and do all kinds of favors, good things, for people.

But on the sad mornings, the mornings that I feel really old, I know that what lies before me are long days, as hollow as dead tree trunks. And that I can do nothing, not even a drop of good.

Running back and forth restlessly, that's been my life since I was a child. Only now, everything is more intense, more powerful, by which I'm trying to say that the happiness and the sadness are also more powerful. And today it is not the big things, but the small ones, the really tiny ones that bring me happiness.

Once it was different. I was happy to be a heroine, to be doing things that no other women around me were doing. May God forgive my soul's arrogance.

On the morning after the dream in which I vanquished the elders, the Maggid sat by himself at the dining table, humming a tune. In the corner stood his aide, Rabbi Feilet, his hands crossed over his chest and his eyes almost closed. When Froumeh came from the kitchen, she called me, "My young mistress!" When the Rebbe wanted me to come sit with him, he also called me this, patting the cushion of the chair next to him. He laid his hand on the back of the chair and, with his free hand, tapped his knees.

"I bless you, my daughter, for the beautiful things you said. You have won the gift of twelve years for my son! My dear one, there is no one like you." He stroked my small child's back. He leaned over to me, his blue eyes radiant, and the sweetness of his words mingled with the porridge I had eaten. I sat up straighter and felt warm and good and sweet.

"How did my master know what I dreamed?" I asked in a voice laden with the chocolate porridge.

"You and me"—he winked—"we already have our past."

I felt the blood rush to my face when I recalled the conversation next to the linen closet.

"And we will yet have the future," he added. A smile suffused his lips and radiated to his cheeks and his eyes. "A splendid future awaits you, Gittel, and it is my voice and eyes that will follow you every moment."

I laughed, reminded of none less than God himself. He enjoyed my laughter, and took up humming his tune once more.

On that morning, a bond was formed between the Maggid and me. I was now one of the ladies of the house. And he was waiting for me the next morning too. So it was every morning: he and I, our chairs next to each other. I had my porridge and he had his tea. I said whatever came into my mind, and he smiled at me with his wide, radiant gaze.

I was his little daughter, his little friend. Rabbi Feilet bowed to me when I passed by, signaling that he was aware of what had happened that night. Rivke'leh kissed my hands and said that I was an incarnation of the biblical prophetess Devorah.

Only my husband—the husband given to me as a gift—knew nothing. And if he knew, he did not say anything. He was silent, always silent. The more silent he was, the more I fluttered and chattered. I learned to flutter from the butterflies in the garden that passed from flower to flower, from one person to another, aimless but for curiosity. As for the chattering, I did not learn that from anyone; the words simply burst out of me like little hummingbirds.

The house was large and always filled with guests. Solitary followers and bands of Hasidim came to us; gentlemen descended from their carriages wrapped in their shiny silk robes; and the poor arrived on foot, their shoes full of mud. They stood in the yard facing the entrance and waited. Rivke'leh offered bread and water to the poor and I helped her. I would catch a whiff of the wagon drivers, the stench of leather, mud, and water, and the scraps of stories—stories that had made them come here—reached my ears, along with glimpses into the lives of the unfortunate, those who dreamed dreams.

They came for a miracle, always for a miracle; the air around the house brimmed with yearning for a miracle. Sometimes, they brought women with them for the Rebbe to help. Paralyzed or mute or afflicted with shaking spells. I would hold their hands and chatter away about the things that I wanted to do or about my dreams or the beauty of the fields beyond the fence. I thought that a yearning for distant things would certainly be familiar to sick women.

And one night, it happened. My husband came into my room, came into my bed, and then I saw clearly that he was very tall and that next to him, I was very little. Lost beneath his body, I bit my lips until they bled.

We did not speak at all, neither of us. He did what he did to me and then he was gone.

His visit was in the dark, and when he left, I was wet and in pain. I lay with my eyes open and I sucked my thumb like a baby. *Is that what people do in the darkness so that there will be children?* I wondered. There was the smell of his body, of sweat, and pain down below as if I'd been cut with a knife. And pain where his beard had chafed my skin.

I lay in the darkness like a corpse and went over and over the thing that had happened. The sounds of my thumb sucking went on in the darkness and the lower part of my body stayed as he had left it, naked and gaping open. A warm and sticky liquid flowed from there and made the linen sheet wet. I sucked my thumb as hard as I could so as not to shout. I didn't light a candle, because I was afraid to see the sheet. He had come to me by stealth, had come in the dead of night, his long, slender body trembling like a feather, and I heard my voice in a low rumble, like a growl, for an instant, I had growled beneath his body. He was shaken by that and his hand had sought out my mouth; he covered my mouth and I bit down. I bit his fingers and he let out a sharp sound. After that he mumbled some things and breathed heavily. And I beneath him, beneath him, hardly able to breathe, drowning.

Why did he hurry to slip away, without any words, like a thief?

The next day, I felt ill and buried myself in bed. Rivke'leh entered my room, wiped my burning forehead, and became very excited. "Now you're a woman!" she said.

I raised my hand and slapped her across the face. Furious that she was happy, I didn't allow her to change the bloody sheet.

"I was robbed!" I shouted.

"You're burning up," she replied.

And it seemed to me that she said, "It's the fever of love." Then I burst into tears.

I said that I wanted to die, and I really wanted to die and really was burning up with fever. I was a child whose body a demon had entered. He was my husband, and yet still a demon.

I shouted, "Demon! Demon!" and smacked myself on the head. My throat was dry, and strange grunting and braying sounds came from it.

Froumeh's red face hovered over me, as did Mistress Sarah's moon face. Women's hands and soft, hushed voices taking care of me, talking around me, falling silent, whispering. I was ill for a long time.

One day, the feather-light hand of my husband touched my hand. He stroked my fingers one by one and said in a hoarse, trembling voice, "By and by you'll be a mother, Gitte'leh, and we will name our boy Yisroel-Chaim." And he said that he had seen it in a dream: me and the boy. I was sitting on a tree trunk that stuck out of the river, the child on my lap.

I did not open my eyes, but I seized his shoulder with my feverish hand and whispered to him that he should never again be silent with me like he was on that night. And I held on until he promised he would not.

Lying there, I went over images of my childhood. And I saw the house, my brother, our journey to Jerusalem together and what had happened after it, and my father and me when he was teaching me to read and the two of us sitting together, poring over Bible stories, and Dasha the servant girl with her stomach that kept growing round and then getting flat again. And the more I recovered and the stronger I grew, the more blurred the images of my old world became. Then it was time to get up, to return to my new life and to throw my heart into it. I was about to swell up, to become as heavy and pale as a goose's egg, and the master of our household, the great Maggid of Mezeritch, was solicitous about me drinking a full glass of milk each morning. With his own hands, he would mix an egg into the milk, hand it to me, and say, "That's for the rabbi that will come out of your stomach, Gitte'leh, so he should be as strong and handsome as our king the Messiah."

And at last, the thing came out of my stomach—that's what I called it, "the thing."

The room was as hot as the fires of hell, and the women sweated and bustled around with bowls of water, and the thing moved inside me, rose and descended and tore my body to shreds. I screamed as I had never screamed in my life. I vomited up my soul as I screamed over and over. I was gasping for breath.

Then they poured water over me and they called out to the Holy-One-Blessed-Be-He. And the Holy-One, blessed be His name, He restored my soul to me again. So that I could scream again and my body could writhe, and the whole room would lurch with me, rising and falling like the wheels of a wagon. A prayer went up from the room that the wagon not get stuck, with me shouting for snow, if only there was snow, if only they could bring me some snow. My throat was parched, my lips dried up, and my arms and legs fell limply, helplessly to my sides.

And then, in the blazing, deadly quiet, it shot out of my body like a ball from a cannon. My head was spinning, and I felt the thing lying there between my legs, making a noise, a kind of mewing sound, and the women sighed with relief. "You have a son, Gitte'leh," they called loudly so I would hear them.

And the thing was there, in the room, among the jubilant women. Only I didn't see; I didn't open my eyes. I lay there, my stomach hollow, my mind empty and hollow. And the thing that was to be my child, that was to be my firstborn son, Yisroel-Chaim, was passed among the women and I was as nothing.

As if from a pit or from a well, that's how the sounds echoed far above me. Weakness enveloped me and I was like a tiny speck within it. I did not open my small eyes, I could not move, and I did not want to move. "You're a mother, you're a mother!" The voices whispered from the top of the well. But I was a little girl, and my mother did not come. I wanted to cry but I did not cry. I was afraid but I did not shout.

I was a tiny grain borne aloft on a strong current, and everything that happened to me, to the grain, was frightening and annoying and not right at all. And the main thing was that I didn't want it and I didn't agree to it. No, I didn't want it and I did not consent to it. Not now, when the thing had come out of my stomach, and not on that night. And not on the nights yet to come. I did not want it and I did not consent to it.

Every night, I was afraid that he would suddenly appear and lie on me. In my eyes, he was a shadow, a spirit that came from the night, and even during the hours of day, he looked like a shadow and behaved like one. We never sat down to eat or talk like a couple. Not even later, when we were a family, did he sit with me and the children like a man does with his family. On the Sabbath and on holy festivals, he would suddenly appear at the table, his eyes veiled, throwing evasive, sideways glances so as not to meet my eyes. And he would cut the Sabbath loaves and whisper, lower his head and whisper the blessings, as if he were in some other place, far from us.

His face was gaunt and sunken, and his red-rimmed eyes protruded. He always looked tired, shut away with his books, his silence, and something secret and blurry hung about him like a cloud.

My husband Avraham was a bird, a bird of passage, who had been fettered to the ground. And I had imposed much suffering upon him when I extended his life.

My births were hard and lonely. The women of the household were there, but it was not my household. Rivke'leh was my friend, but her mother Froumeh kept busy with housework. It was a Hasidic house, and rabbis, disciples, and simple folk came and went all the time, which meant there was always much work. As for Mistress Sarah—she was the queen of ice! And Froumeh reeked of sweat and cooking; and there was a fat midwife, who kept sighing and blowing her red nose on the white towels that she used for the birth. They kept touching me, watching over me, arranging the linens around me. All the while, my head just stuck out from beneath the white sheet as if it had been severed from my body and left there to cry and shout.

And when my stomach gaped open, my heart did not open but rather closed. At my first birth, my heart hardened and closed. At the second birth, it seemed to lock completely because I was so weary of being nothing but the bearer of my husband's sons.

When I held my firstborn son, Yisroel-Chaim, I knew that he would be neither king nor messiah. He was a large, quiet baby who liked to eat. He sucked dry my small nipples and then went happily on to the nipples of the wet nurse.

One year later, my younger son was born, Shalom-Schena, and this time nothing could be taken for granted any longer. I was now aware of life's complexity. I looked at this new baby; he had large eyes as black as wells, and a weak, slender body. There were many nights I prayed for him to live till morning. And when it was light, and when the golden rays of the sun were entangled on the bed quilt, he lay breathing next to me, flushed with the pain and effort of the night, or stretching out his arms to me, trembling and fragile and crying out with fever.

I would curl my body around him, and a wild joy set my soul ablaze. I stroked his dark head with its huge eyes and told him stories.

Here is our righteous Messiah going alone into the forest; a carpet of leaves rustles beneath his feet. Here he is sitting beside a pool in a forest clearing, casting his line and fishing for the souls of particularly beautiful children. And the fishing rod has a red hook, and its catches will grow up to be righteous or very wise men.

I went on to tell him about the city that King David built at the top of a mountain. And how the drought in the Land of Israel did not touch the mountain, how rain fell only on the city and there was desert all around it, and how they built the Temple at the edge of the mountain. And the Gate of Mercy that leads to it. And afterward, when the Temple was destroyed, the gate remained standing where it was, strong with its curved arch on top.

And how, one day, the Messiah will come through that gate on his white horse, riding to the ruins of the Temple, and he will search among the stones for the hidden holy spark. And when he finds it, he will light the flame anew, and light up the innermost hearts of the Jews. And everyone, the poor in their rags and the rich in their carriages and the crippled and ill leaning on their sticks or carried aloft on their sickbeds, all will stream toward the holy mountain.

I can see those years before me: I'm a girl of fourteen, I'm fifteen, I'm sixteen, running across the fields of Vohlyn with my older son behind me. He takes slow, careful steps, and my younger son is in my arms.

And then my sons are toddlers, running ahead or following behind me, and the soft air of summer caresses our faces. There's a heady scent and vast open spaces, and the bodies of my children are warm in the sun. The rays of the sun not only warmed my body, but warmed my heart, which had hardened after the births. And soon my protective love for my fragile little son melted me.

I shout, "Blessed be You whose world is so pleasant!" The boys roll in the soft grass. And I pull my kerchief from my head and a wave of warmth suffuses my shorn head.

When my sons grew older, they began, one after the other, to study Torah, and my elder son joined the world of the men and was lost to me. He prayed and he studied, and when he was around me, he lowered his eyes and was silent. Only my little son continued to run with me in the fields; only my little son, Shalom-Schena, the four fringes of his undervest whirling in the air around his lean body. Only he would throw himself down next to me in the tall, soft grass, and his black eyes would open wide when he heard my stories.

Only he threw his skullcap off his head, as I did with my headscarf, and the two of us were like Eve and her son in the Garden of Eden. The two of us alone, all by ourselves in an abandoned kingdom. And there were no laws in our kingdom. He was a prince and I a queen in the Land of Dreams, a land of earth and trees and tall grasses and a light, playful breeze.

My little son, Shalom-Schena, was almost nine years old when I handed him over to the men in black. I told him that I was traveling to the city atop the mountain, in the heart of the desert. I said that, one day, he would come riding on a horse, and pass beneath the arches of the gate. And I told him that if he came, he would surely search for the hidden spark amid the ruins. Lies, so many lies . . .

He pleaded with me to stay, even talked to me about a match—marriage with Rabbi Nachum, his teacher—but I refused. I was conscious that a young Jewish widow in my position could not remain unmarried and independent for long. But I felt an intense resistance to returning to the life that I had already lived. My husband Avraham was dead, but he visited me in my dreams and tormented me, sternly warning me to stay a widow. And all this pushed me toward the dreams I had in my childhood, of the kingdom that awaited me in the east. I would not consent to losing it again, and I thought of nothing but running away.

Life is a journey of loss. First, I lost my father and my mother, then I lost my husband, and then I lost the land of Vohlyn and my two sons. Nothing was left to me but a dream and I followed it. And when I reached my dream, I lost it as well. The mountain was a hill, and instead of a holy city, I found a group of wretched houses filled with sick, desperate people.

When I came here, I blotted out my past and my name. I am only Gittel, the washerwoman, and I hear the voice of God in my loneliness. He speaks to me and breathes His light, even breathes to me, giving me tranquility.

The repose of God is with me instead of this poverty and suffering. At first, I also suffered; I was sick and my soul wished to die. But He who heals the sick and straightens up those who are stooped, He stood before me and infused me with breath, and since then, I have been stronger than all my ailments.

Health looms large in a city that swarms with disease. Those who are healthy are afraid of the sick, those who are sick hope for a miracle, and the fear and the fervent desire for a miracle can turn even a washerwoman such as me into a healer. I know nothing about medicine, but on good days, when the spirit moves me, I am ready to say a prayer and to lay my hands on the sick.

And they come to me with their infirmities. At first, it was only the Arabs—only the poorest of the poor and the sickliest of the Ishmaelites. After that, Jewish women started to come. And now, even respectable people make their way to me in secret, clandestinely, when no one can see them. I do not ask them for payment, only that they give something to charity.

Once, an Ishmaelite claimed that I had bewitched his son. The Ottoman guards came to exile me from the city. I took two plates, a knife, and a prayer book, and left my home.

For a long time, I lived in the fields outside the city. I lived like a creature of the fields, picking fruit and drinking water from the spring. At night, with my knapsack on a stone and my head lying on the knapsack, I slept like our father Jacob with all the stars in the sky traversing above me in song. Yes, those were nights when I could hear the singing of the stars, and during the day, I sang their song as I sat in the shade under a tree.

Then, one day, a couple came to me, lepers from the colony to the west of the city, asking me to heal their son. They dragged their child behind them; he was wrapped in a filthy cloth. He was shouting wildly, in a clear, piercing voice, and he hid his thin arms, covered in sores. I sang to him and I asked him to sing with me. While we were singing, I took off the filthy cloth, and when he was naked I washed him in the waters of the spring. Then I instructed him not to drink any water unless it came from that spring. That boy was granted healing.

After that, the villagers came to me, seating themselves in front of me in the field, under the tree, waiting for a miracle. I told them I was a washerwoman and if they would give me work, I would pray for them. They gave me clothes to wash, and I prayed for them. And so, very slowly, I was drawn back into the company of human beings.

One of the Ishmaelites prepared a room for me in a small village outside Jerusalem and I lived there for some years. On the Sabbath and on the days of the holy festivals, I would clothe myself in white and walk back to the Jewish quarter in Jerusalem. The village people called me "the Jewess" and "the enchantress" and put me on a donkey for the journey up to the city. Their life was simple and their eyes were always turning to the east, to their God.

I felt good living with them; even my loneliness felt good. After several years in the village I went back to live in the city, among my Jewish brethren. Man is like a fruit—he belongs to the tree on which he grew. And for us Jews, our tree flies in the air. Its roots are up above and its fruit touches the earth, but is not quite connected to it.

Since my return to the city, I have a room and a rooftop. The room is shadowy and the rooftop is open to the skies.

I do laundry on the roof; I sit on the roof at sunrise and at sunset, climbing up and down the narrow stairs that spiral upward. And cats and dogs rub by my legs, wailing for food. And doves and sparrows congregate above and chirp for food. I scatter grains, and toss pieces of bread soaked in chicken broth.

The animals came here from the village. They followed me just as Ruth the Moabite followed her mother-in-law Naomi. The birds have come from the skies. Animals can sense a solitary soul and they cleave to it like a man cleaves to his home.

In my sleep, I sometimes hear the sounds of geese and ducks, and when I wake, I think I'm back in Vohlyn and that, by and by, I'll hear my mother's firm step or Dasha whistling to the fowl in the yard. Of late, my legs are heavy and a longing for the sounds of my childhood lingers with me.

One day, a Hasid came to me with his barren wife and said that he had been a disciple of Rabbi Shalom, the grandson of the Maggid, and that, since the young rabbi died, he had decided to set sail to the Land of Israel with his wife.

Up to that moment I was standing. Then I sat down.

The Hasid wiped his eyes with the edge of his *kapote* and said, "My beloved Rebbe, Shalom-Schena, was different from other righteous men. He would wear regal purple garments adorned with gold, but on account of the puddles and mud on the way to the *beis midrash* where we studied, he preferred to study in his home. It was in Froibich—even the name of the place gives me the shivers. We were a small group, perhaps some ten young men around him, serving him like the heroes of David. And he would tell us how, at night, he sat next to King David, their chairs touching, with David singing and playing the harp and revealing secrets to him. The splendor of his clothes and the splendor of his house were part of his secret, and we felt that each movement we made and each word we spoke might elevate us to the highest temple or send us down to the world of ashes.

"The external world is the gate to the spark within, like a temple within a temple, that's what the Rebbe said. That's why he held beauty and order in the highest esteem. And his wife also walked about like the daughter of a king at home, and serving women brought their food in splendid vessels. He and his wife sat at one table, while we sat at another table, lower than theirs.

"Even now that I am in the Land of Israel, praise God, I long for my Rebbe's soft feet, encased in chamois leather, treading quietly, floating, with a fine scent trailing in their wake, accompanying them . . . O, my Rebbe looked like a prince!"

A sigh escaped from the Hasid's sunken chest. Because of the heat, he wore his garment open, and stains of sweat and of something yellowish, perhaps soup, could be seen on his robe. I saw all this as I sat, mute, on the chair. His barren wife kept standing in the doorway, not raising her eyes from the floor. The Hasid moved around the room, distracted, agitated. One moment, he sat down on my bed without asking permission and, a moment later, he jumped up, blushing, and returned to pacing the room, his arms crossed behind him.

"I saw how he died," said the Hasid. "Like his father, the Angel, he was slightly sick, and then suddenly he was gone.

"For a few days, he was pale and lay in his regal bed, spitting blood into a bowl. And he summoned his child to him, and said that he had seen himself in a vision. And in his vision, he sat in the temple in the sky. On the table in front of him was a splendid crown, a holy crown formed of letters from the Torah, but he was not permitted to put it on his head. The Rebbe laid his hand on the head of his son, and then he coughed and withdrew his hand, turned his face to the wall, and his soul departed."

The Hasid again wiped his eyes with the fringe of his caftan. He tugged at his nose as he said, "That's how my Rebbe died."

What I said then, if I helped cure his wife, and how they left, I have no recollection—only that, after a time, I found myself alone in the room.

Only now did I know I had hoped one day he would come to Jerusalem. Only now did I know I had been waiting for him, that I'd had no doubt we would meet again. And now the dream I had secretly harbored had died, the dream that I had hidden even from myself had died. My younger son had died.

I began to pray to him, to pray to the child of almost nine I had given over to another's care. I saw his face at that time, going to study with Rabbi Nachum and then returning to me, coming back to me. For years, I had not heard his voice, and now his voice came back to me, speaking from my womb.

We were still running, he and I, in the fields. We were still removing our head coverings, standing tall, without shame, without sorrow, in the eyes of God. We were still running, he and I, and suddenly I stopped. I stopped and fled. I fled from my son and I did not look back.

My cheeks burned with shame, but this time I faced my thoughts: I didn't run from them. I had betrayed my younger son; for the first time, I uttered a word to myself: *Traitor.*

For the first time, I looked at his sorrow. How he had fled Rabbi Nachum, and fled again, and again. And said that Rabbi Nachum did not understand his soul at all. That was how he said it: "He does not understand my soul."

Everything had been concealed, everything suppressed. The sorrow had been concealed beneath his face, the shame beneath mine. And he said that no one understood him like I did. And I betrayed him. And when someone betrays you, their words no longer have value. I said, "Go to Rabbi Nachum. From now on, he is your home."

My eyes filmed over and beneath them, deep beneath them, my shame was concealed.

But now, years later, the thin film was torn. My eyes saw it all, how it was back then, when he was only nine years old. And remorse, sharp as a blade, pierced my heart.

Remorse has been tearing at my heart ever since. There is no way to escape the pain, not ever. No amount of light can dispel the darkness of remorse.

The colors of the Vohlyn countryside were gray and black. Black was the color of the men, the color of funerals, the color of the vultures that filled the skies. And gray was the everyday color, the color of the homes and the air inside, the color of the women's dresses, the color of mud, the color of the forest when you were lost inside it. And at the edge of the grayness and blackness of life, there were streaks of green and silver. The fields were green, and amid them, the rivers wound like silvery snakes. And gold flickered on the heads of the young women, gradually turning silvery like the rivers. And when there was a storm, the lightning flashed and the gray clouds blackened, and the color of the Day of Judgment spilled down on the castles of the lords and the huts of the peasants.

And the Jews fled home to lock their doors. And they wondered if this was the day when redemption would come. And redemption was the color of Jews, white and pale like goose feathers. Swaying. Rumbling. Redemption was like the palm branch we wave on the Festival of Tabernacles.

When I left Vohlyn, I followed the road to redemption.

I walked south down the muddy roads that follow the River Bug. Barges floated on the river, as did heavy logs with peasants astride them, singing and laughing. Geese also drifted on the river and large birds, their wings outspread, flew above. The birdsong and the sounds of singing and laughter were lost in the tangle of vegetation that wound to the right and the left like silent walls.

The vegetation burst through to the water, and floated on it with branches laden with leaves. Roots spread over the water like nets. Sometimes, a musket shot would ring out, and after it, the silence hung even heavier.

Villagers passed me, stooped beneath bundles of wood. I spent the nights in their huts for a meager sum. They bowed before me and crossed themselves when they heard I was on the way to Jerusalem. *"Ohhh!"* they said in wonder, and at night, they hid small wooden crosses in my knapsack.

The farther I got from Vohlyn and the nearer I came to the Black Sea, the more the colors changed; they became brighter, clearer.

Through the trees, large expanses of sky could be seen and the river grew broad and indolent. There was more marshland and clouds of buzzing insects hung in the air. Instead of the huts of villagers, there were now summer cottages. I traveled in wagons and, at night, I slept in inns.

Sometimes, I met Russian pilgrims who were also making their way to Jerusalem. The women talked to me, touched me, and smiled at me from toothless mouths. But I felt uneasy with their intimacies and kept slightly aloof from them. There was something frightening about the bands of pilgrims. They dragged feet wrapped in rags, held pinewood staffs in their hands, and their eyes shone feverishly like the eyes of the sick.

A terrible smell rose from the marshes and clung to my nostrils. The smell stayed with me when I crossed the broad Dniester River as it wound its way to the River Prut. There, I saw a group of women bathing in the river and I joined them. They had black hair like myself, and they were lighthearted, shrieking like doves. And when I took off my dress, they stared at me curiously and spoke among themselves in a strange language.

I saw that, around their necks, they did not wear a necklace with a cross and, with hand gestures, I asked them who they prayed to. "Allah!" one of the girls told me, waving a wrist covered in bracelets to the sky.

For the first time in my life, I was with Muslims. Their colors were new to me: brown and ochre, earth and sun. And when I bade farewell to the women and continued on my way, the awful smell was gone. My body moved lightly under my dress and the tinkle of their gold bracelets resonated in my ears.

The journey south, to the shores of the Black Sea, was like crossing a rainbow. Colors and languages were constantly changing. Women in colorful clothes mingled with men all in white, soldiers resplendent in shiny boots passed in open carriages, plump merchants stood by the roadside hawking their wares. Vagabonds loitered by the side of the dusty roads and begged for alms in the doorways of the inns. Sometimes, there was rejoicing and dancing in one of the village squares; sometimes, a bear stood there tethered with a chain and surrounded by a crowd.

The village squares with churches and those with mosques began to blend together as I walked. Sometimes, processions went by headed by priests carrying a cross, and sometimes, the sounds of Muslim prayer echoed in the air and the men fell to their knees and brought their foreheads to the sand.

And I was like a black ant amid a sea of color. I was like a fleshless shadow among the merchants and the vagabonds, amid the drunks and thieves. I slept in rooms for simple folk, as quiet as a mute. And perhaps my eyes also burned like the eyes of the insane, but I could not see them to know.

The vapor of Your breath, God, is what carried me along the rivers, past towns whose names I did not know. It is what drove me forward until, one morning, on a wagon full of goats—they were crouching around me, bleating, and I kept clicking my tongue to hush them—I saw far ahead, far beyond the fur hat of the goat merchant, towers and domes of gold. The merchant said, "Istanbul," and the goats clung close to my knees, fixing me with their watery eyes and bleating.

They were drawing closer to their death, while I was drawing closer to the largest city I would ever see.

～

Istanbul was a beehive with swarms that flowed toward her with a mighty buzzing. In Istanbul, I found synagogues and Jewish homes, and sat facing a Sephardic rabbi, reciting prayers in Hebrew so that he would know—despite my nomadic appearance and my black headdress, in spite of the rancid smell of goats—that I was still a Jewish woman.

I told him in Yiddish that my husband had died and I was making my way to Jerusalem, and to my surprise, he understood and took me to his wife, the *rebbitzen*. When I stood in front of the woman with her wise eyes and her face the hue of an olive, my knees shook because I was hungry, weary, and had been isolated from my own people for so long. My voice faltered when I said, "Have pity on me." Then I fell silent and I left it for her to do as she pleased.

The *rebbitzen* gave me her protection. She fed me and took care of me and now, for the first time in many months, I ate at a table where all the blessings were said. Around the table sat her five children, boys and girls, and the singing of the boys on the Sabbath brought tears to my eyes. I saw that she was scrutinizing me and wondering what I had been through and where I had come from, but I didn't tell her anything. Only that my name was Gittel and that I wished to reach Jerusalem.

When she heard the word "Jerusalem," she said that first I had to get stronger. And that it was not a good time to sail there. It was because of the rabbi's wife that I stayed in Istanbul for several months and became a washerwoman.

I washed clothes in the homes of Jews and Armenians in the neighborhood. On the Sabbath, I ate at the rabbi's home and, on religious festivals, I went to synagogue.

Once again, I heard Jewish melodies and Jews praying.

My benefactress found me a room in an attic. The window of my room reflected the tongue of blue water that breaks forth at the Black Sea and almost ends and yet does not at the vastness of the Great Sea that leads to the shores of the Holy Land. I was surrounded by the colors of light and sea.

My life in Istanbul was like the calm before the storm. The quays from which the ships sailed stretched out under my feet, the dockhands loaded and unloaded freight, and sailors strung out ropes, climbed masts, and shouted at the top of their lungs like cranes. White waterfowl filled the air with their mighty cries, and it seemed as if everyone was constantly shrieking, the fowl and the people and the ships.

And even though the water was moving, it seemed to stand still. I sat on the windowsill at sunrise and again at sunset, though in truth, I was also in motion, on my way to another place.

One day, a small boat dropped anchor at one of the quays. It was blue, with white sails. The sunlight made its white sails look golden and its blue hull bobbed on the water's surface like a large fish. On the side of the bow, its name glinted in letters I could not read, and next to the name was a painting of a woman with a fish's tail. There was no one on deck. The wood planks of the deck were polished, and the ropes were coiled into barrels. When I returned to my room in the evening, the ship blushed in the light of sunset, and I imagined myself standing on the deck facing a golden shore fringed with palm trees, my feet bare and my hair fluttering in the breeze.

And just as the boat had appeared, so it disappeared. The sun went on shining as always, there was the usual commotion of porters and birds, but where it had been moored, only water glimmered. I searched for a small blue stain slipping out between the ships, but saw nothing.

Meanwhile, winter came and the colors changed. The tongue of water grew grayer and strong winds whipped up froth from the turbid waters. The white birds disappeared; the ships were shrouded in black cloth and huddled close to the quays. The alleys looked narrow, as if they had suddenly shrunk, and in the nearby shops, wood was sold for heating.

At the festival of Hanukkah, I lit a menorah on the window ledge; water seeped into the attic and gusts of wind made the flames of the candles dance. A young man arrived at the rabbi's house from Poland. He was a goldsmith and seeking a bride. The rabbi's wife with her olive complexion rolled her eyes heavenward and said, "Mysterious are the ways of God. Perhaps He has sent this fine man because he does not wish you to reach the Holy Land."

I remembered how my husband had visited me in dreams after his death and asked me not to marry anyone; how angry he was when my younger son wanted to make a match between me and his teacher, Rabbi Nachum; how Avraham came to my son in a vision at night and shouted, "Who dares to enter my antechamber!" And now, my husband was back again, appearing in my dreams, all in white, almost transparent, gazing at me silently and shaking his head.

With my attic room so cold and damp, I spent many hours at the rabbi's house. My limbs grew plumper and rounded out; the goldsmith caressed me with his eyes and sang Hanukkah songs in his deep voice. And yet I could not shake off the injunction of my dead husband,

and I could not cease to think of Jerusalem. Istanbul was like a lighted room, with soft Ottoman chairs, and the good Jews walked about and whispered softly in my ear. I lived in the Jewish quarter, in an attic surrounded by the sea and sky, and something rose from inside me, opaque as dust.

Sometimes, at night by the window, caught in a flash of lightning, my skin was reflected back in the glass, gleaming. The solitude was immense, but it was not everything. There was something else in my heart: there was pain that pierced my flesh from the inside, and my reflection in the glass shone with that pain.

The pain was love. In Istanbul, a painful love bloomed in me, faintly luminous. I no longer had a choice, but had to resume my journey, to follow Him.

Toward You, after You, in the radiance of the morning rays of light and in the sadness of sunset. Toward You, after You, Lord of the East.

Winter was drawing to a close.

The first birds passed on their way north, homeward, and the quays slowly returned to life. Men swathed in hoods rubbed golden oil onto the ropes and the sides of the ships. Barrels were loaded into the fishing skiffs and nets mended. And in the splendid parks around the homes of the merchants, plants spilled out of the curling arabesques of golden railings. In the shaded stores, there was cleaning and polishing in preparation for the festival of Passover and, in the house of the rabbi, on the night of the Seder, all the branches of his crystal candelabra were lit and their light spilled over my face.

And one morning, with warm sunshine on my face, I boarded a ship bound for Jaffa. The rabbi's wife stood on the quay and waved her white handkerchief. I looked up and saw the attic window where I had lived, and above it, the tower that reared up over the Jewish houses. An expanse of blue, growing ever larger, separated me from them. The tower pushed out over the water like a solitary finger, erect against the sky, and when it faded into the distance, the last thread that linked me to that land was severed.

I stood on a moldy deck, reeking of fish, and a special feeling, like before a wedding, washed over me and grasped at my throat.

"Blessed art Thou, O Lord, for plucking me from the shore and bringing me onto a ship. Blessed art Thou, for Yours are the seas, and the delicate shards of froth that are sprayed on me are from Your robe. You are my only Lord, enclose me within the palm of Your hand like a ship within a ship, look down from on high and see me sailing in Your hand, sailing toward You."

And all my longing and all the beauty of a new country were reflected back to me from the waters around the ship. An Ishmaelite stood by the ship's wheel, his huge belly before him. His fleshy, mustachioed, pockmarked face was chewing, chewing and spitting out a kind of sticky dough like the Turks' sweet locum paste.

And all my longings gathered about me on the deck as I breathed in the smell of fish. And a cry like the sound of a bird leaping from its nest burst from my throat, but no one heard. The sailors were busy, and the handful of other travelers also stood on the deck and gazed at the water, deep in their own journeys.

On the way, we stopped at ports in the Greek islands and bought bread and fish. And at every port, I fantasized about disembarking and getting lost among the sunburned people who smiled from their blue wooden boats—lost among the vines and the olive trees and the tiny white houses.

Throughout the day, I stared at worlds drenched in sunlight, and by night, I dreamed of Istanbul. I see the large drawing room in the rabbi's home, and the gold merchant smiling at me. All his teeth are made of gold and sparkle in the candlelight. Then I am sitting on a chair like the Prophet Elijah's throne with a goblet of wine in my hand, and the wine spills over the rim and stains my white dress. And the rabbi's wife shrieks like a bird, flies above me, and covers the stains with her hands. Above her head, wrapped in a sort of turban, I see the laughing face of the merchant, with his glinting teeth dropping out of his mouth like orange peels. And my ears are filled with a loud piercing sound, like the noise of fowl running wild, and it fills the room and deafens me.

In all the dreams, there was a great commotion, and the rabbi's wife and the gold merchant always appeared. And I tossed and turned on my bunk in the belly of the ship, while snores rose in the darkness from the other bunks. I'd wake drenched with sweat and my clothes gave off an acrid smell.

There were lice on the ship. They leapt on me and crawled over my skin and made my life a misery. Like some mangy street dog, I kept scratching myself, and the worse the situation became, the more light there was in my dreams of the rabbi's drawing room, the guests milling around as beautiful as angels, and the goldsmith rising up among them, his face beaming like a star.

As I lay back down on that bunk, I wept, scratched myself and wept, and I begged the evil inclination to leave me in peace. Every night, at night's end, I would go up on deck and collapse, as weak with fatigue as if I had just come through a lengthy battle.

The Ishmaelite stood next to the ship's wheel, his large body dark in the starlight, and an immense dread, blacker than black, possessed me and did not leave until the light of dawn.

The nights rent my soul and the days patched it up. In the days, the sea was blue and all kinds of fish jumped out of it and disappeared back into its belly. And once again, I knew where I headed, and the evil spirits of the night receded. There were a handful of Jews with me on the ship, among them a Hasid, dressed in fine clothes, with his maiden daughter. He reminded me of the mystical Baal Shem-Tov, Rabbi Yisroel ben

Eliezer, who set out for the Land of Israel with his daughter, Adèle, and they were attacked by bandits and endured all kinds of hardships until they were forced to return to Istanbul.

The Hasid's daughter was mute. She sat on deck with her legs splayed out and gazed at the sea. Sometimes, she seemed to be seized by demons and her body would shake violently, her fists drumming on the deck as she wailed.

Her father sat next to her in a chair, reading, and when she began to wail, he would get up and stroke her head and shoulders until she was calm. They slept in their own cabin, and on the Sabbath, they came out to stroll on the deck, once in the morning, and once in the afternoon: she in a purple velvet dress and he in a silk robe and with a fur *shtreimel* on his head.

Apart from the Hasid and his daughter, the Jews on our ship were poor and their clothes were worn out. They spoke the language of the Turks, sat cross-legged on the deck, chewed dry bread, and chattered in their tongue. Three times a day, they stood to pray, facing the east. The Muslim captain and his sailors prostrated themselves five times a day, also facing east.

The east was like God, hidden and instilling dread. He was hidden in the distance beyond the blue water, far off behind the horizon, and yet He was also with us, sailing with us from sunrise to the rising of the moon.

The east was the port to which our prayers were sent, where the birds migrating from the north flew, where the prow of the *Galata*, our merchant ship, was headed, named after the tower in Istanbul. And at night, when we went down into the belly of the ship, a handful of sailors would stay on deck.

On our last days at sea, an easterly gale began to toss the ship. A layer of dust mingled with sand coated the deck, filling our nostrils and becoming entangled in our hair, painting the world a grayish yellow. It was as if the desert had conquered the sea, pushing our ship back.

Get you gone! Turn back while you still can! The wind roared, wrathfully whipping off head coverings and slapping our faces with its dry hands. The Hasid gripped his book between his knees, shielding it with his hat as his beard fluttered about his face like a flame. Eventually, he closed the book and closed his eyes. An expression of suffering crept over his face and his lips moved in a whisper.

His daughter sat at his feet, enchanted by the wind. She tipped back her head, opening her mouth wide and gulping it in. Her black hair came loose and covered her face, and she laughed as it lashed against her forehead. She shook her hair again and again as she tipped back her head with a kind of wild delight.

The group of eastern Jews pulled their capes tight around themselves. With their turban-swathed heads, they looked like pears, and when the time came to pray, they stood and swayed, the capes billowing around them like wings. And when their prayers were finished, they folded their wings and sunk to the deck, waiting for the fury to abate.

Restlessness assailed me and I could not sit still. Dust irritated my eyes and my entire body itched. I was thirsty, and the stagnant water that they gave us did nothing to slake my thirst. My stomach was churning and my legs wanted to walk, to run, to flee the tossing ship, the wind screeching in my ears, and the menacing sense of the east getting ever closer.

Here it comes, my stomach shouted, *it's coming now—this thing I've been waiting for all my life!* I paced the deck and soundlessly pleaded that this thing would be good. That it would be His will, His good will, pouring on me from above when I finally disembarked from this wooden vessel and entered my ancient-new country.

There is no fear greater than the fear before disembarking in a land you have dreamed of. All the hardships of the journey drain into one immense fear, as sharp as an arrow. Before I alight upon it, the land is a secret that whispers in my ear, an enigma suspended above my head like a sword, and there is no escaping it, nothing to do but sail forth and face it.

It was only once in my life that I sailed to a new shore. The mist of the hours before casting anchor, the stupor brought on my fears of what was to come—I recall them as clearly as I recall my dead and my children.

It is with the same sharpness that I recall my first sight of the Land of Israel, one large blur separating into trees, houses, boats. And the colors—the yellow and brown, brown and gold. The houses are few, and gray; the boats gray and few. At first glance, the trees seem to have no leaves, but upon closer inspection, they are date palms with long fronds.

Sight is the start of everything and after it come the voices, the scents . . . the touching.

Only once in my life did I touch a new shore, on a fresh, clear day, rising up as if it had been born out of the sandstorm.

In the morning, the sailors washed the deck and the passengers rose from the dark entrails of the ship, relishing the clear air and the smooth sea. The poor Jews from the east sprawled sleepily in the sun on the damp deck, their bundles spread out around them. The father and his daughter, freshly washed and dressed in their Sabbath clothes, sat down on their large iron chest. He held her hand in his, both of them looking numb.

I paced back and forth along the railing, running my heads over the peeling paint. Leaden distress weighed on me, making my muscles twitch. Nothing had passed my lips since the sandstorm, and hunger, anguish, and anticipation for the coastline that had not yet appeared made the last hours torturous. My leather knapsack hung from my shoulders and in it was the little prayer book, the siddur from my father's home.

And when the land rose from the horizon and was still one lump, brown and long as bread, I thrust my hand into my bag and felt around for my prayer book. It was my home, my talisman, the only remaining evidence that I was who I was.

The lump rose from the sea, it rose like a primordial monster, and all the prayers and the legends and the pilgrimages I had heard of encircled the land like a cloud and I could not see it the way it really looked. The tension exploded in my chest, pulling my body downward. Had I not gripped the railing, I would have fallen.

Now of all times, when the sea voyage had come to its end, I began to drown. I drowned in the bare skies, in the furious light of summer; I drowned in the great desolation that went on and on, inland, to the hills and the desert.

At the moment I touched this land, I knew I would never leave it. That never again would I board a ship; that I would drown in this land for all eternity.

Now, throughout the nights, by the sparkling light of a candle, I sail from port to port in a colorfully adorned ship, facing the wheel. People board my ship and disembark, the living and the dead; time inhales and exhales, engulfs and spews up, until there's no distinction between Vohlyn and Jerusalem, between past and present, life and death.

And now my ship is sailing into an old story. The Maggid, beloved of my soul, told me this story, his face aflame and, all around it, his white hair standing on end.

Years before I was born, Rabbi Yisroel, the Baal Shem-Tov, set out on a journey to the Holy Land. He left his home with his daughter, Adèle, and a disciple whose name was Rabbi Zvi the Scribe. They reached Istanbul in the winter, but they could not find a ship traveling to the Holy Land. They stood on the shore and the Baal Shem-Tov took a handkerchief from his pocket.

"I shall spread my handkerchief over the water," he said to Rabbi Zvi, "and you must think about the name that I will tell you. If your thoughts wander from it for a moment, the three of us will be lost at sea."

He was ready to spread his handkerchief over the water, he was ready to set out upon the waters, but Rabbi Zvi caught hold of the handkerchief and refused. In the end, they hired a boat, but a storm broke out. Lost, the Baal Shem-Tov, his daughter, and Rabbi Zvi washed up on a desolate island.

Then out of the wilderness, out of the blue, some brigands appeared and attacked them, and took them prisoner. Bound in fetters, Rabbi Zvi said, "Now is the time for a miracle, you must save us."

The Baal Shem-Tov replied that all his powers seemed to have been stripped from him.

Rabbi Zvi realized he had also forgotten everything apart from the letters of the Hebrew alphabet.

The Baal Shem-Tov shouted, "So then why are you keeping silent? Say the letters!"

Rabbi Zvi began to recite *"Aleph, bet, gimel . . . "* and the Baal Shem-Tov repeated the letters with great enthusiasm, nearly snapping the fetters from his hands. He had almost managed to break them when there came the sound of a bell. An old captain appeared with a band of soldiers and released the captives.

When the three of them reached Istanbul again, the Baal Shem-Tov understood that heaven would not permit him to travel to the Land of Israel, and he returned home.

"That is holy devotion!" said the Maggid in wonderment. And he placed his hands on the table and said that, if the heavens wished it, then right at that very moment, he and I would travel to the Land of Israel. For a while, he kept his fingers pressed to the table, then let them drop and sighed sorrowfully, *"Oy!"*

I thought of the morning when we could have traveled to the Land of Israel, when the Maggid's court moved from Mezeritch to Rovno. It was a day of great commotion. Froumeh bustled around me shouting about spoons and plates and no one had any idea where they were, my children trailed after me crying, tugging at my dress, and two wagons laden with furniture and belongings stood opposite the front gate. Next to them were two rented carriages, one for the women and the other for the Maggid and his entourage.

I never understood why we were compelled to move.

At that time, there was much talk about gentile armies drawing nearer to us, there was also talk about Jews who plotted against us and sent informers to spy on us. Young men stood in the courtyard, whispering secrets, and when the Rebbe showed himself at the window, they were greatly moved and the words "It's a miracle" spread like fire in a field of dry thorns.

Everyone waited for something extraordinary to occur, something that would change the laws of nature. But nothing happened, only that suddenly the men talked about moving, and they spent a lot of time arguing in the courtyard about where the Rebbe should move to and what this meant. The Maggid's gout had become much worse. He seldom left his room, and when he did, he dragged himself about on crutches, Rabbi Feilet supporting his waist.

Instead of coming to the table, he would call me to his room to drink tea with him. I would carry in the tray while he waited for me on the tall sofa, his wasted body lost inside it, his legs wrapped in a blanket. Behind him was Rabbi Feilet, always standing guard.

In his room crammed with books and medications, the Rebbe said, "Rovno, there is no choice but to move to Rovno."

And he said that while sipping his scalding tea through a cube of sugar under his tongue. His sick hand trembled and some of the boiling water spilled on the blanket, and the silent giant behind him raised his bushy eyebrows, signaling that I should slip away.

But the Maggid narrowed his eyes and examined me with great attention, until I could see the delicate threads of veins in his eyes and the watery light blue color that surrounded his pupils. Then he let his head drop and sunk into the solitude I knew so well, the solitude of those with great thoughts and of tall mountains that touch the clouds.

While Froumeh was packing, Rivke'leh and I often ran off to the hills weeping together because she was about to be married and would not be coming to Rovno.

On the day of the move, she stayed very close to me, and I held her chapped red hand in mine. The children straggled after me, and Shalom, who was finding the change difficult, buried his face in my dress and would not stop crying. The young men in the Rebbe's court buzzed like a swarm of bees. Peasant men and women from the surrounding villages came to bid us farewell, thick-bearded men who stood outside the fence fingering their caps and their fair-skinned women whose children climbed the fence. The commotion grew and grew until it suddenly ceased.

There was utter silence when they brought out the Rebbe. He was seated on a folding bed, his hands on his knees, his eyes half-shut. Then his hands floated up to bless all those gathered. The peasants bent their backs, bowing to the holy man, and the young men of his court gathered closer around his bed. Rabbi Feilet pushed the bed and ignored the large crowd.

The door of the carriage was opened, and the attendant hoisted the bed with the great man in the air as if he were a small child, and then the door closed and the curtain was lowered.

A long sigh of relief, of longing, of finality, went up from the crowd. A few women wailed quietly. Froumeh parted from her daughter with instructions and warnings about what she should do. The red fingers released my fingers, grew farther from me, waved good-bye, and we were off.

My husband, Rabbi Avraham, was not with us that day. He had traveled to serve as a rabbi in a place called Fastov. I had two children, I was the princess at the court of a great rabbi, but my husband was not with me. Sometimes, he would appear in the forecourt, self-contained and distant. We would sit in the dining corner and he would glance at the children, then at me, quickly lowering his gaze when I looked back. And all the time, he was fearful, his voice low and hesitant, glancing around nervously, as if I might devour him, heaven forbid!

The years in Rovno were the Maggid's last. His body weakened and, when we sat together for tea, I would help him drink from a spoon. Sometimes he would ask me about my husband, calling him "my only son" and saying incomprehensible things like, "Never muzzle an ox when it is threshing" or "The rope went down after the bucket."

Rovno is situated at an important crossroad. It is a city of bustling alleys, of fine ladies and gentlemen, and I had nothing to do in it other than slowly suffocate. The fields were far away, having retreated to the surrounding hills. The noise of passing wagons and carriages could be heard from the house, and the house itself belonged to an influential local man and had a large reception chamber and a stable in the forecourt.

In the abandoned stable, I kept chickens and geese. I made myself a corner among the animals and spent the mornings there with my younger son, Shalom. He was not yet studying Torah, his curls fell onto his pale, round face, and he ran joyfully about the stable. At first, he was afraid of the shadows and gloominess and the odor of horses that hung in the air, and he would lie on me and scratch his flea-bitten legs the whole time. Very slowly, he discovered the haystack and the water pump, and stopped scratching himself. He got used to the smell and made himself a corner next to my corner.

We would bring along bread and milk and we would play make-believe, him and me, about all kinds of things. For example, that I was a queen and he was my royal son, or that we were birds. I would tell him all kinds of legends I'd once heard from Dasha, my old servant, about the house I had lived in as a girl, about the Garden of Eden. He sat in the corner he'd made for himself, a little fort of chopped firewood, his eyes wide open as he listened to me and sometimes closing as he drifted off to sleep.

Once he told me that, when he grew up, he would be an angel. I thought about his father, who was called the Angel, and I wondered what could be detaining him in Fastov so long after the holy days. I felt sad that our son hardly knew his father at all.

Even inside the house, Shalom would follow me everywhere. Once there was a baby bird he loved to cradle and carry around. Froumeh shouted that I was spoiling the child and made a big fuss until the Maggid intervened and said that I was right. He stood up for me because he felt indebted to me. He never forgot his role in arranging my marriage. He said, "For me, there is no question: Gittel is right, she is always right. On no account I can come to her with complaints."

When he had gone, Froumeh said that the Rebbe was spoiling me just as I was spoiling the child. I did not know why exactly, but I knew that it was on account of Avraham that he always defended me.

Rabbi Avraham's shadow seemed to hang over me even when he was far away. And even after we returned to Mezeritch and the Maggid died, the shadow of my husband did not allow me to live my life.

We went to Rovno to escape the armies of Napoleon as they were moving across Europe, and we returned to Mezeritch after a few years because the Maggid's health had deteriorated. He said it was his wish to die in his old home, in Mezeritch. We returned as we had left, in carriages and wagons, but in complete silence and with no crowd to greet us.

When we returned to Mezeritch, the broad expanses of the wet fields were spread out before me like a mantle. I gulped down the chilly air and was overwhelmed with bliss. I hugged Shalom, my son, and told him I had forgotten how much consolation there is in nature.

And I went back to roaming about the fields, sometimes alone and sometimes with Shalom. He had begun to study Torah, but was not completely immersed in it like my firstborn. He still stayed close to me and would only leave me for short periods of time.

The Rebbe also returned to his old room. His doctor lived with us now and took care of him constantly. The faithful Rabbi Feilet slept on the floor in front of his door, and liked to say that he relished the role of a worn-out doormat.

Rivke'leh, a married woman now, cried a lot about not yet having a child. I asked the Maggid about it and he said her wish would be fulfilled after his death. And indeed, one year after he died, her first son was born and he was named Dov Ber after the Maggid. Rivke'leh compulsively examined his leg, fearing it might become paralyzed like the Maggid's. By the time I left for Jerusalem, she already had two sons and one on the way. And every year, she would travel to the grave of the Rebbe and hear him telling her that her eldest would always be healthy.

In the Maggid's last days, Yisroel-Chaim returned home from the yeshiva where he was studying. He was thin and pale, and I devoted myself to making sure he ate. When the Maggid's soul left his body, I was with my two boys in the dining room.

We heard a loud scream. Yisroel-Chaim leapt from his chair and ran to the bedroom. When he came back, he said that Rabbi Feilet was shouting that the Rebbe was dead. I gathered my chicks to me and I did not know what to do. I shouted out Froumeh's name and got no answer. I began to wail and little Shalom joined me.

Then people started coming, more and more people. Rabbi Nachum's flushed face, wet with tears, leaned over my sons. He whispered something to them and they followed him. I dragged myself to my room and lay on the bed, inundated with the voices of men reciting psalms for the dead. The following day, my husband arrived and seemed shrouded in darkness. He asked that the windows be closed and sat on the floor facing the wall.

A large crowd assembled and filled the wooden stairs. We shut the doors and, behind them, we could hear restless noises. When the dead man was brought out, the crowd burst into a great moan. I saw my husband covering his face with his hands, and after that, everyone dispersed and the house emptied out.

I went outside alone. I sat in the field waiting for the day to pass and sunset to come, but before the sun sank low, I went back inside to prepare the house for mourning. And I felt very sad to have missed the sunset that day.

The Maggid died and I stayed in his house. We stayed, me and my two sons, and Rabbi Feilet, and Mistress Sarah, and, of course, Froumeh. Mistress Sarah's mind was no longer clear. Froumeh kept her washed and fed while I supervised the kitchen.

The Rebbe's long-time students came to pray and to talk. My husband also sat with them, but he was silent the entire time and looked completely devastated. After a while, he again set out for Fastov, where he served as a rabbi.

He would occasionally come back, but his absences grew longer and longer. I was married and yet I lived like a nun. My husband had no interest in our sons, but the Maggid's students took them under their wing. Yisroel-Chaim did not return to the yeshiva. His body grew stronger and his cheeks ruddy.

Rabbi Nachum, in particular, would visit us often. He was squat and rotund, with a pinkish face from which bristles of white hair stuck out like feathers. He talked a lot with my sons, in a loud voice and gesticulating, and when he spoke, his eyes would follow me.

In our home, glances were the language beneath words. Rabbi Nachum talked to me in this language and I answered him in kind.

~

At the end of the year of mourning, my husband asked me to come to live in Fastov, and I said no. Important people and dignitaries came to rebuke me for not following my husband, but I was firm in my resolve. I could not tell them that I was angry with my husband and that it was on account of this anger that I would not go to live in Fastov.

Besides, I had grown to love the spacious wooden house with its windows that overlooked the fields, and I could feel the Rebbe's spirit there. Sometimes, I even saw him as if he were alive.

When he appeared before me, I told him what was in my heart. He would remain silent and look at me, and then I would know what I had to do. I talked with the rabbi's spirit about Fastov, and as I was talking with him, it became clear to me that on no account would I go to my husband. I was too angry with him.

Exactly one year after the death of the Maggid, six days before the first candle of Hanukkah, my own father, Meshulum Feivish, died.

It was the depth of winter, and the roads were all covered with treacherous ice. The gloom of the forests held sway over the world and, with it, an immense quiet, broken only by the wind's howling. It was in this dangerous quiet that I traveled to Kremnitz, to the home of my dead father.

Here I was, parting from my children—my son Yisroel-Chaim, serious and obedient, holding Rabbi Feilet's hand, and my younger son, Shalom, livid with anger, heartbroken, running after the wagon screaming. And on this journey, all alone, the quiet reminded me of my nuptial journey: my mother next to me, the scent of perfume, and the blue skies. Now in the opposite direction, my heart was as hard as a stone and I just could not cry.

Once, my father was closer to me than anyone. Then, that fateful day, he'd hidden in his room with his holy texts, peering out the window as I was taken away, and I never saw him again. I opened Ecclesiastes and read aloud to myself, and the words accompanied me all the way back to my parents' home.

I did not cry even when we came into Kremnitz. And when I descended from the wagon I was alone. I raised my eyes to the window of his room and, for a moment, I saw his face, peering out at me as he did then. Again I was a girl, a stubborn, wise girl. My father taught me Torah, but he would have taught me more had I been a boy.

When I went up to the veranda, Dasha came toward me, fair and plump. A huge wave of smells engulfed me, and I buried my face inside her bosom with its coarse linen apron and, at long last, I wept.

I never wept so much as during the days of mourning for my father. I wept for my childhood, for the fact that I was not a boy, for my early marriage, for a husband who was not and had never been with me, for the children I had left behind, for my brother who estranged himself from me after our failed journey to Jerusalem. I cried for my mother who still ruled the house with an iron hand, but looked older than I remembered and would speak of the same things again and again.

My father, Meshulum Feivish, was a renowned Torah scholar, and so from far and wide people came to weep over the wisdom that was no longer. In my eyes, my father resembled the wise King Solomon, and like him, he sat and studied and saw and understood. And when he died, his death was like the death of a king.

Next to the house, a large mourning tent was set up, and rabbis dressed in black delivered eulogies and spoke words of Torah. My brother Mote'leh also spoke, and I saw him the way he had been when the two of us went to Jerusalem and I could not stop crying.

After the seven days of mourning, I found I could not leave. I had returned to my old home, to my father's books, to the crowded kitchen with my mother and Dasha, and it was like returning from a long exile. At night, I slept next to my younger sisters, together with them in the soft, wide bed, and at dawn, I heard Dasha clucking to the fowl in the yard. Still in my nightgown, I would run outside; I could not help myself but ran to her, trembling with cold.

My mother scolded me from the kitchen, "You're still the wild creature you used to be," and for a short while, I really did feel wild, with feathers and fur, and I forgot my children and my husband and the mourning that hung over the house.

One day, a messenger came and said that my husband was waiting for me to return. Without wanting it, I returned. I loved the house in Mezeritch and I loved my children, but still I wept all the way back to them.

And yet, a death even harder than the others still awaited me—the one I had vanquished as a young bride. Now I was a married woman, an angry woman, and I did not heed the signs that warned me of what was to come.

Almost three years had passed since my father died, and things were tranquil in Mezeritch. Rabbi Nachum had sent a tutor for my sons. The man lived in our home, under the watchful eye of Rabbi Feilet, and on festivals, he would travel home to his young wife. Yose'leh was his name, and he was a strong, healthy young man who used to carry the children on his shoulders and play with them like a big brother. The Rebbe's large library was their classroom, the open fields their playground.

I looked after the family, cooked for them, and when important guests came, I looked after them. The Rebbe's friends and students did not cease to come, and money also did not cease to flow, always through Rabbi Feilet's pocket. From time to time, very infrequently, the children's father would appear and their voices became hushed. Yose'leh would take a stick and bang it on the table, and the boys would be obedient and study harder, lowering their heads and keeping silent whenever their father entered a room.

This father of theirs, like a great black angel, passed through the rooms and conversed with Rabbi Feilet, touching the Maggid's books, and when I served him food, he would peck at the plate and not look at me. When he did look at me, I saw that he was angry I had not gone to live with him, but the anger was tight within him and had no outlet.

Sometimes, he would knock on my door and come into my room, looking around long and hard, as if to stamp it on his memory, and then he would gaze out the window or say something that never amounted to a real conversation, then blush or go pale, as if he had glimpsed something painful. I might say something about the children and he would make clucking sounds with his tongue and pull at his earlocks, quoting from the Song of Songs—"My dove in the clefts of the rock," or "How beautiful you are, my beloved"—then shuffle his shoes against the floor as I kept silent, waiting.

But nothing, nothing ever took place between us that was like the Song of Songs, and he would slip away as he had come. It was not clear to me why he had come. And after he had gone, I would be filled with insult and anger.

My birdlike husband, who looked as if he were lost, as if he were wandering the face of the earth. My husband, who took flight and had fled his father's royal court, his children and me—my husband who had been sentenced to death, who on my account had been granted a stay of execution—was without protection for the first time in his life. I was told that, in Fastov, he shut himself away in his room, almost without food, and when he went out, he frightened his congregants with his silence and his pale, hollow face. Strange stories about his behavior reached my ears. They said he would hide his face in a scarf when speaking to people, and when he was praying in the synagogue, he would beat his head against the wall.

But for us, in Mezeritch, summer was rampant, running wild. Yose'leh and my sons took their books out to the meadows, and I went back and forth between the house and the meadows. I drifted from the large shady kitchen to the wide-open windows, from the windows to the verdant trails that led to the river. And in the depths of thickets and the reeds that grew by the banks of the water, I threw off my clothes and dove into the clear water.

The insects buzzed close around me that summer, and the chickens and the geese I kept in the yard clustered close around my ankles. The dishes I cooked were so rich and tasty that Froumeh said that an angel must be helping me. The children's cheeks filled out, their voices grew deeper, and their skin was tanned in the sun and looked soft and smooth.

Even Shalom, my sickly son, was healthy and elated that summer. In the evenings, he would tell me legends he had read in the Talmud, about kings and wise men who lived in the Land of Israel, and he painted the land in gentle, soft colors, which today I know are not its colors at all.

At the end of summer, my husband came to us, appearing suddenly as was his wont, only thinner and even more silent than usual. He did not come into my room, did not approach the children, just shut himself away in the Rebbe's old room and asked Rabbi Feilet to bring his meals there.

And on the eve of the Sabbath, when my husband was still with us, the Maggid appeared in my dream and ordered me to let my husband know that he should exchange his room for mine, or at the very least, he should move his books to my room. In my dream, the Maggid stood upright, not crippled or limping as he had been in his lifetime, and his pale eyes were wide with undisguised anxiety. I immediately tried to tell my husband. I knocked on his door over and over, but he did not open it. I told Rabbi Feilet I had a message for my husband from his father, but he came back, saying Avraham was immersed in prayer and refused to hear a word, so the opportunity was lost for me to deliver the Maggid's warning.

The evening after that Sabbath, a fire broke out in Avraham's room and consumed all the books. There was a huge commotion in the house. Rabbi Feilet dragged my husband from the burning room, and all of us carried buckets and ran to put out the fire. Yose'leh, the boys' teacher, was the hero of the evening. In his white nightshirt, his eyes shining and his muscles visible in the firelight, he threw blankets on the flames and gave instructions on where to spray the water. Rabbi Feilet, the boys, Froumeh, and I ran back and forth with blankets and buckets, but my husband just sat at the kitchen table, his shoulders drooping and his skin blackened with soot, as rigid and solitary as a statue in the desert.

Even when the fire had been put out, he did not bestir himself from his numbness. He merely wrapped himself in the dressing gown Froumeh had brought him, his body shaking with the cold. And when it was dawn, he slipped away, back to Fastov.

The High Holy Days approached. The dignitaries of the Maggid's court, who had urged me to move to Fastov, returned to scold me for not going and even blamed me for the fire.

"You are a rebellious woman," they said, and one of them, whose name I do not wish to utter, made a gesture of contemptuous revulsion and almost raised his hand against me.

I was weary of words, weary of everything that had happened, and I threw all my energy into cooking for the festival. A day before Rosh Hashanah, the last messenger from my husband came, requesting that I come for the holidays. Again, my soul's dear friend came to me in a dream, his hand floating upon my head like a tiny ship, and in a gentle voice—the voice in which he had spoken to me at the very first, when I emerged from the linen closet—he said that if I didn't want to, I should not travel to Fastov. So I did not join my husband.

Yose'leh's wife came for Rosh Hashanah, and Rivke'leh and her family were also with us. The skies were full of clouds and fresh autumnal winds shook the windows. Large flocks of birds passed on their way south. Throughout these festive days, I gazed at my two sons, and it was as if I were discovering them anew and I became aware of how much I truly loved them.

Yisroel-Chaim sang the festival songs in a strong, pleasant voice; he ate and sang and his pale eyes shone. Next to him sat his younger brother, his black curls falling over his eyes and his soft mouth as round as a red ribbon. He was wearing the velvet coat and silk pants I had sewn him for the occasion. When he caught my gaze, my younger son fluttered his eyelashes and pulled down his mouth like an old rabbi, blowing air through his lips while still fully concentrating on the prayers.

My princely son, I thought, *there's greatness in your face, but only I see it, only I see it so clearly!*

That day, I felt the immense happiness of discovery within me. I saw the biblical Hannah and her son Samuel beside her, dressed in a cotton robe. Then my imaginings blended with the smells, the colors, the dishes, the songs, and the blessings of the New Year.

For a moment, I remembered my husband, and then forgot him all over again. Far from my sight, he was far from my heart. A dozen years had gone by since I had fought the heavenly court on his behalf. Now I did not want to fight and I did not want to remember. And letting him slip from my memory was the true beginning of his death.

Yom Kippur, the Day of Atonement, also came and went. Rabbi Nachum arrived two days after the festival, and as was his custom, he took the boys to synagogue all day. But unusually for him, he avoided my gaze and kept away from the dining table. He admitted that an important matter was troubling him, but did not explain, looking fixedly at his fingernails so as not to look at me.

On returning from afternoon prayers, he closed himself in a room with Rabbi Feilet, and immediately after that, he set out again.

The following morning, the children rose before dawn and rushed to the synagogue. I was especially surprised by Shalom, who normally found it difficult to get up and always sought a pretext to stay in bed.

On the third day, I followed them to the synagogue, and from the window, I heard them recite the mourner's Kaddish.

I took my younger son aside and shook him fiercely. He burst out crying and said, "Mama, we're orphans!" And he said that Rabbi Nachum had warned them not to tell me.

I rushed back home and pounced on Rabbi Feilet.

The man covered his head with his hands, but let me go on shouting. Eventually, he said that Avraham's followers had decided not to tell me he had died because they found it difficult to deal with me, and more difficult still to admit they had failed to protect my husband.

"Difficult?" I roared. "What about me, isn't what's happening difficult for me?"

I never shouted like that, like I did at Rabbi Feilet that day. I shouted that they did not have enough respect for me, and asked how they could have drawn my children into the conspiracy—the orphans of the dead man—how they could forget that I was the widow, that I was the one who had tried to warn about everything that was about to happen. My husband had never listened to me, and they had never listened to me, and now they had conspired to cheat me out of my mourning.

It was as if I spewed some disgusting reptile from my soul, and after my tirade, I was left weak and spent, but it was clear to me what I must do. I tore my dress as mourners do and then sat down on the floor till the seven days were over. The days that remained of the week of mourning were mine, completely mine.

Women from across the region came to comfort me. Rivke'leh tended to me just as she had in the days when she was unmarried. My sons repented their sin toward me and the three of us curled up together on the floor, sharing warmth at this time of unraveling, the end of the old home, the end of the Rebbe's court. It was the end of my marriage and the end of my sons' lives under my wings.

What can a mouth say apart from whispering love?

Who will I love but You, my Lord? For You are Lord of the secret wind that bears my body aloft in the night, Who takes me far beyond the four rivers to a forbidden garden, wonderful and lost.

A great, expansive quiet engulfs the garden. And solitude closes my mouth, so the words are forgotten, making me tumble down to Your feet. Take me, take . . .

Everything that happened after the death of my husband happened slowly, without a plan, and step by step brought about the revolution in my life. I heard the word "revolution" from refugees who came from the land of Ashkenaz. They spoke of turmoil and war and destruction that had left their land broken and fragmented. And yet that devastation paved the way for something completely new to arise.

"That's revolution," they said. "It's the end of the old ways to make way for a new path."

When did the house begin to collapse beneath my feet, when were my sons lost to me, and when did I know that I had been left utterly naked? Time blurs in my head and there is no forward, no backward, only darkness and radiance.

The darkness lasted many days.

First, I closed up the Rebbe's old home; I closed it up and sold it. I sold furniture, clothes, books; one item after another from my matrimonial home. I wore a market apron, as my mother had worn, and I took a stall in the marketplace in Rovno.

Again I lived in this city of merchants that squats in a valley. My sons still had beds in my home, but the study of the Torah took them from me. They moved to Chernobyl, to the home of Rabbi Nachum, two days' distance from Rovno, in a large house I had never seen. My son Shalom often talked about that house. He spoke about Rabbi Nachum's many disciples and about his way of talking and joking around a simple wooden table, the rabbi dressed in old clothes, telling stories about the wise men of the Land of Israel who were carpenters, shoemakers, and farmers.

"He's a man of the earth," said Shalom with an adoring expression. "He goes around in galoshes and the hem of his coat is always muddy."

My son Shalom, so different from his Rebbe, was delicate, his clothes always fine, like the son of a king. He would comb his curls around his face, keep a folded handkerchief in his shirt pocket, and take care that his clothes were always clean and pressed.

He would often leave without permission and travel to see me. I would come home, smelling of the market, and he would be sitting at the table with a holy book. He would wrinkle his nose at the smell and say, "How Joseph missed his mother Rachel" or "How David suffered when he fled from the fury of Saul." He saw himself as the righteous Joseph and as King David. He saw himself longing and suffering as they did.

I would be exhausted from a day of standing at the market, and yet I still stood and cooked and we sat down to eat. My son sat facing me, as handsome as Joseph, as beloved as David, and the room was bathed in radiance as I gazed at my child's dreamy eyes and slender fingers.

Tears filled my eyes and fell onto the food, so even the food was radiant. And it was as if a splendid dome rose up over us, as if we were cut off from the world. And a kind of quiet descended and drove out all the weariness and grief.

My son would stay awhile with me, and the radiance remained between us all those days, and when I went to the market, I would long for my son and would hasten home as early as I could. That was how it would be until a messenger arrived from Rabbi Nachum, and on a few occasions, he came in person.

Then there were the looks, those meaningful glances that always passed between Rabbi Nachum and me. And when the rabbi came my son would go silent, mute as a fish. And I'd pack his laundered and pressed clothes, fold the handkerchiefs, and wrap up some pie in a cloth, and then the two of them would set off.

My son would leave, holding Rabbi Nachum's large hand, then the radiance left my house. The darkness would fall upon me. It loomed over me even when I was standing at the market stall, my lips moving without a sound, counting the money that, one day, when the hour of the revolution came, would allow me to travel to the Land of Israel.

At night, the darkness also held sway. And from within it, there rose, sparkling, the faces of the dead. The face of the father-in-law who had been so kind to me, and the face of my father, and the face of my husband. The Maggid taught me how to treat people and how to earn money to support myself and my family. My father pushed me to remarry, and warned me about haughtiness and the evil spirit. My husband claimed that I was his, that I would always be his; he said that the thread that connected us would never be severed.

The words of the dead confused me and I didn't know what I should do. In the meantime, I saved up some money and sewed silk garments for my children, and in my heart of hearts, I yearned each day to come home and find my younger son waiting for me like Joseph for his mother, Rachel.

And without noticing it, I began to think of myself as Rachel. I thought that perhaps I would also suddenly disappear from my sons. I would not die, but leave and not return to them.

I was deathly afraid of these thoughts—what mother thinks of leaving her sons and not returning? Nevertheless, I was unable to banish the idea.

So I buried myself in work. I was the first to open her market stall in the morning, and in the evening, I did laundry and sewed and sank into a deep sleep. But in the middle of the night, the dead would again begin speaking in my head, and again I would hear the voice of Rachel, which really was my voice, saying to me, "Be on your way. Leave the boys, leave everything and take up the wanderer's cloak."

And when I heard that voice, I grasped my head in my hands and I begged it to be silent.

I think back to that time, in Chernobyl, that winter when the wife of Rabbi Nachum died. Before he started to court me. The snow had come and a great unbearable cold took hold of my life. I was in Mezeritch, the Maggid's hometown, quite alone after the deaths of my father and father-in-law, and hardly saw my sons. To keep my soul alive, I read stories from the Bible.

Again I saw them walking toward a distant land, fathers and mothers, and children small as stars, accompanied by sheep and camel. And it was as if I, too, walked in the hot, soft sand, as if I were part of that large family, from the same tribe of nomads.

It was as if the land had been waiting for me, and I sank into it, slipped between the grains of wheat and sand, and it felt good to me, good. The silence at home was immense, the distant land was close, and again I was able to go toward it as in my childhood dream.

So winter passed for me, in hard work and in a great dream.

And when the snow melted, my young son appeared again, his face full of stories of Rabbi Nachum, about the goodness of his heart and his happiness. I listened to him and I saw the distant land slipping again out of my reach. I felt my solitude afresh, and I told him that I had no roots in this place, no home of my own. And when he heard this, his face fell and he said, "If we could only travel, just you and me, to a distant place!"

So I spoke to him like a mother and I said that he had to look to his own life, and to thank God that Rabbi Nachum cared for him and guided him.

And he said that Rabbi Nachum did not understand him, did not understand his feelings.

And there was silence between us and I did not know what to say. And afterward, he remained at my home for a few days and there was an atmosphere of sadness over us. And when he had already packed his belongings to return to Chernobyl, he suddenly turned to me, his face reddening, and said, "Why don't you marry again? Why not marry Rabbi Nachum?"

For a moment, I thought, *Yes*. I recalled the looks between us. *Me and him. Me and him and the boys.* And a clear picture of a real family. And a leap in my heart.

The magic made me dizzy.

But then, the shadow came and laid its hand on my heart. My husband's hand, the one I'd felt on the nights I do not want to remember. My body began to shudder and I was unable to breathe.

My son was alarmed and fluttered around me, saying something about a queen locked in a tower. And that night, his father the Angel appeared to him, his face as black as coal, standing on a roof and shouting, *How dare you bring a stranger into my house, into the house of the dead?* And my son awoke from his sleep and told me about the dream. And I comforted him and I said that nothing could be done.

After that night, we both accepted our fate and what was to come.

I knew that I would never marry again. Shalom returned to Chernobyl to wed the daughter of Rabbi Nachum.

~

He was a child of almost nine, whom with my own hands I gave to a man who did not understand his feelings.

And there he stood dressed up like a groom, as if for the Purim carnival. At his side stood a girl in a wig, a wig with braids, and a veil over it.

He had lost his father. He did not know it, but very soon he would also lose me. And I stood next to the bride, who had lost her mother.

I am a widow in a black dress, and on the other side of the wedding canopy stands Rabbi Nachum, dressed in a festive white robe. He is also a widower, and above us there is an awning of white silk.

We stood there, me and my small son, and my elder son was also there with us. Yisroel-Chaim was ten years old and he was also engaged to be married. I wanted to hold them both, my two sons, and to wrap them in a white cloth, to swaddle them in it as if they were babies. But I could not do what I wished.

My own will surrendered to other things.

I looked into the eyes of my son, the groom, and saw that his will was also overcome.

He sat with Rabbi Nachum over the *ketuba*, the marriage contract, and the rabbi laid his large forearm on his shoulder and drew my son to him. My son must surely have felt he was being crushed, and must surely have smelled the wine Rabbi Nachum had drunk in honor of the occasion. But he was silent and did not run away.

And the little girl bride, what was she feeling? What did she know?

Her mother had died the previous winter. And my son Shalom was full of dreams.

He wore a white headdress like the one—he said—the Messiah would wear. They were both orphans and they were wed. They were husband and wife.

And I had a stall, I worked like a dog, and I dreamed about a far-off land.

No one knew my dreams, no one knew my longings, only I knew that very soon I would part from everyone. I would even part from my children and I would never see them again.

The wedding glass was broken and my heart was also shattered.

Every parting is a shattering, and my heart was in pieces. I looked at the glass wrapped in white fabric and I heard it breaking. I heard the shouts of happiness. Facing me were a boy and a girl, and the boy was my son. He was my younger son, and soon he would never see me again. He would have an adopted father who did not understand him. And this matter of understanding is delicate and elusive. This matter of comprehension complicates everything. And what would my son think of me? For there was understanding between us, but now he would cease to know me. Even if he wished to and tried with all his might, he would never understand.

Will he hate me? It's a question that I should ask in the past tense. Did he hate me then, when I left him all alone?

And if my sons spoke of me, what did they say?

And even worse than this was the possibility that they did not say a single thing. Nothing about me, about me leaving, about what might have befallen me in my new place.

Now, when I am old, I do not know if I am still a mother. Or why it hurt me so much when I heard that my younger son had died.

A wedding at joyous Purim, but a wedding full of sadness. The groom in the miter of the Messiah and the bride with a wig plaited into braids.

A wedding is the happiness of the living and the dead, of the dead mother of the bride and the dead father of the groom, who was called the Angel. A wedding full of sadness, death waiting to ambush us all. And the dead do not rest, but descend and move about the world. And the world was created by the hands of God, so it is written in the holy books. And those holy books are the threads that connect the living with the dead.

My father, Meshulum Feivish, was a great Torah scholar and he loved the sacred books. He loved me, his daughter, but would have loved me more had I been his son.

When I met the great Maggid, I already was his daughter-in-law. My soul was entwined with his soul and, while he was alive, I had a home in the world. When he died, my home was destroyed and I was left exposed.

After that, my husband took flight; he did not die but spread his wings and took flight. Surely he is sitting now on the chair which once I saw empty.

At the age of twelve, a short time after my marriage, I ascended in a dream to the Sanhedrin, the mystical Jewish council, and I presented arguments to them which I did not remember afterward. My father-in-law, the great Maggid, saw what happened and remembered it all.

He knew me far better than I knew myself.

He was a man with splendor, with a light that touched the hearts of human beings. And since he died, I have not seen any such splendor in the world.

Once I thought that I would see many people like him in the Land of Israel, but I was very wrong.

People here are like people everywhere, only poorer and more lowly than those outside the Land of Israel.

When I arrived here, I fell sick, and while I lay on my deathbed, I heard the voice of God. Since then, I see the glory that lies under the pain. Glory hides under the abscess, it glints through crumbling stones and from the dry earth cracked open by thirst. And the people, and the land, they are as one dough. And glory hides inside it like a raisin, like sweet dried fruit.

When I was a girl, I held my brother's hand and we set out walking to the Land of Israel. Many years later, I reached it alone. I entered my childhood dream and I never left.

My lifetime was divided into two: wakefulness and dreaming. When I set out on my journey, it was like sinking into a deep sleep. I forgot the respect that I had been given, the family that I'd had, and I was no longer concerned about earning a livelihood. In my sleep, I entered a deserted land, I laid my pack down on its ground, I laid my head on a stone, and I lay in the field. And I heard a voice calling me: "Gittel!" And I saw a ladder.

There was no one climbing it and no one descending it. It stood alone like a palm tree, the sun glinting between its slats, and by night, the stars.

A terrible sorrow engulfed me upon seeing it. I sat at its feet, and I wept.

A creature of the field came up to me and I stroked its head. After that, people came to me and I stroked their heads. And slowly, slowly I felt gladness seeping into my hands. And that happiness filled my veins and choked my throat.

The happiness burst from my eyes and the ladder looked different to me. It was rustling with life.

My words are the words of a dream. They fly like wild bees from place to place, trailing drops of honey, hovering aimlessly in the blue air.

EPILOGUE

When I put down my pen, Gittel left me. In her place was my great-grandmother with her wrinkled face and her toothless mouth, smiling among the trees.

And my home was in Jerusalem with its gray sky, adorned with miracles. And my great-grandmother disappeared in the trees. I waved to her and she whispered, "Who are you?"

And Gittel was no more, and my great-grandmother vanished, and as for me, I returned to a shady corner in the garden of writing.

ABOUT THE AUTHOR

Born in Tel Aviv, Smadar Herzfeld initially came to Jerusalem to work with underprivileged children. She is the founder of 62, a boutique publishing house that specializes in books on women and religion. Herzfeld, who writes about characters with strong spiritual and religious beliefs, has penned four novels and a book of poetry. Her novel *God Isn't Me* won the Jerusalem Foundation Award. The mother of two adopted sons from Vietnam, Herzfeld lives in Jerusalem. Learn more at www.publishers62.co.il.

ABOUT THE TRANSLATOR

Aloma Halter is a writer, poet, translator, and editor. She was born in London, studied literature at the University of Cambridge, and came to Israel in 1980.

Halter has translated four novels by Aharon Appelfeld into English, including *The Story of a Life,* and edited many novels, which include recipients of the Koret Prize and the National Jewish Book Award. Her edit of her father's memoir, *Roman's Journey,* was acclaimed in *Publishers Weekly.* She lives in Jerusalem with her two daughters.